"Jealous?" Gabriel stopped, blocking the path.

About to do the whole "excuse me and why would I possibly be jealous?" bit, I remembered my vow. No more pretense. No more lies.

"Jealous as hell," I said.

"Good." And then he kissed me again, taking his time about it. He'd kissed me before. Hot and hard. Cold and sweet. This was different. I'd never been kissed like *this* before. It was as if he was giving me a part of him that he hadn't even known existed, and something so deep inside me that I'd forgotten it was there responded and answered him with everything I had to offer.

And then there was a clatter of feet and the dogs, stupid things, came careering out of the woods, expecting to be told how brilliant they were.

Gabriel held me for a moment, face as grave as it had ever been. Then he took my arm, tucked it beneath his. "Let's go pick out a Christmas tree."

Dear Reader,

Quiet, studious Ginny Lautour and Sophie Harrington, privileged, lively, the class "princess," were the two girls least likely to be friends. But Sophie's natural kindness in rescuing a lost soul on her first day at school, and clever Ginny's aptitude for getting Sophie out of trouble, forged the kind of bond that lasts a lifetime. So when Sophie begs for Ginny's help to save her job, even though it means breaking into her sexy billionaire playboy neighbor's apartment, she doesn't hesitate.

And everything would have been fine if Richard Mallory was—as promised—away for the weekend. But then Sophie wasn't being entirely honest with her best friend. She wasn't in trouble. Just matchmaking!

As Sophie discovers, however, when you tell a big fat fib, even if it is with the best of intentions, it's likely to come back and bite you. Homeless, jobless and with Ginny honeymooning with her beloved Richard, Sophie has no one to turn to. For the first time ever she has to live on what she can earn and, with Christmas coming, the only job on offer is that of dog walker to gorgeous grouch, Gabriel York. But it's the season for miracles and once he offers her a home, no matter how temporary, all things are possible.

I do hope you enjoy reading how best friends Ginny and Sophie find their very special happy endings in *The Billionaire Takes a Bride* (#3817) and *A Surprise Christmas Proposal* (#3821).

With love,

Liz

A SURPRISE CHRISTMAS PROPOSAL

Liz Fielding

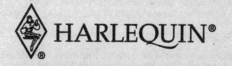

HARLEQUIN®

TORONTO • NEW YORK • LONDON
AMSTERDAM • PARIS • SYDNEY • HAMBURG
STOCKHOLM • ATHENS • TOKYO • MILAN • MADRID
PRAGUE • WARSAW • BUDAPEST • AUCKLAND

ISBN 0-373-03821-6

A SURPRISE CHRISTMAS PROPOSAL

First North American Publication 2004.

CHAPTER ONE

'WHAT kind of job are you looking for, Miss Harrington?'

'Please, call me Sophie. Peter always does.'

And where was Peter when I needed him? I'd been bringing my untapped potential to this employment agency for the last five years. Dropping in whenever I got bored. Or when an employer decided that I wasn't quite what he was looking for and encouraged me to widen my horizons. As far away from him as possible. Or when he decided that I was exactly what he was looking for and wouldn't take no for an answer...

Actually, on this occasion I'd quickly realised that I was never going to be what my present employer was looking for, so, although it wasn't a good time for me to be out of work, I'd taken pity on him and done it for him. Now, confronted by the frosty-faced female on the business side of the desk, I was beginning to wonder if I'd been a bit hasty.

'Anything,' I said, finally cracking in the face of her silent refusal to pick up my invitation to engage in social interaction. Get some kind of relationship going. 'I'm not fussy. So long as it doesn't involve heavyweight typing or computers. I've had computers up to here.'

I touched my forehead with the tips of my fingers

to emphasise just how far 'up to here' with them I was.

Then I smiled to show that, computers apart, I wasn't going to be difficult. I couldn't afford to be difficult...

Like my expensive manicure, it was totally wasted on this woman. Unmoved, she said, 'That's a pity. Your experience at Mallory's would seem to be your most promising asset. What kind of reference would they give you?'

That was a tricky one. My interview technique had involved nothing more taxing than flirting at a party with a software boffin who had, apparently, been in search of a secretary. I'd never actually been a secretary—and I'd told him that—but I'd been prepared to give it my best shot. And he, sweet man, had been prepared to let me. Now, there was a man who appreciated well applied nail-polish...

Unfortunately perfectly painted nails and good eyelash technique, even when coupled with the ability to make a perfect cup of coffee, hadn't entirely compensated for my inability to type with more than two fingers. Especially since, attractive though he undoubtedly was, flirting had been as far as I was prepared to go.

To be brutally honest, I'd only held onto the job for so long because his boss, Richard Mallory, had been about to marry my best friend. I'd brought them together through some seriously clever matchmaking and Rich hadn't quite been able to bring himself to invite me to take my skills elsewhere—which was why I'd made everyone promise to keep my resignation a secret until they'd left on their honeymoon.

He'd found out somehow, but I'd kept well out of his way during this last week before the wedding. Right now I needed a job—really needed a job—but not so badly that I'd watch a grown man break into a sweat as he tried to persuade me to stay. And I wouldn't be asking him for a reference for much the same reason.

I'd given it my best shot, but I'd missed the target by a mile. I was never going to be secretary material.

'I tend to do better in jobs where social skills are more important than the ability to type,' I admitted, avoiding a direct answer to her question. 'I've done reception work,' I offered helpfully, indicating the thick file that lay in front of her. It was all there. Every job I'd ever had.

'Presumably in the kind of reception area that doesn't involve the use of a computer,' she replied, signally unimpressed.

'Unfortunately they're few and far between these days,' I said, and tried the smile again. In the face of her total lack of encouragement it wasn't easy; this would have been so much less difficult if I were talking to a man—men, simple souls, took one look and tended to forget about tedious things like computers and typing speeds. But I wasn't sexist. If she'd just give me a chance I was prepared to work with her on this. Really. 'I worked in an art gallery once. I enjoyed that.'

Well, I had—until the gallery owner cornered me in the tiny kitchen and I'd had to choose between unemployment and taking my work home with me. That had come as something of a shock, actually. I'd been fooled by his fondness for velvet trousers and satin waistcoats into believing I was quite safe...

'Lots of opportunities to meet wealthy art collectors, no doubt. We're not running a dating agency, Miss Harrington.'

If only she knew how far she was from the truth.

'I don't need a dating agency,' I said, possibly a little more sharply than was wise under the circumstances. But I was rapidly losing any desire for interaction of any kind with this woman.

I didn't have any trouble attracting men. It was convincing them that I wasn't in the business of making all their dreams come true that was the problem. The ones who worked it out and still wanted to know me became friends. The others became history. Dates I could manage for myself. What I needed was a job. Now.

'I usually see Peter,' I said, offering her a way out. 'If he's in? He understands what I can do.'

The look I got suggested that she understood, too. Only too well. 'Peter is on holiday. If you want to see him you'll have to come back next month. But I doubt if even he would be able to help you. Companies are looking for function rather than adornment in their staff these days.' The woman indicated the file in front of her. 'You've had a lot of jobs, Miss Harrington, but you don't appear to be actually *qualified* for anything. Do you...did you ever...have a career plan?'

'A career plan?'

For heaven's sake, did this woman think I was a total fool? Of *course* I'd had a career plan. It had involved an excessive quantity of white lace, two rings and a large marquee in the garden of my parents' home. I'd started working on it from the moment I first set eyes on Perry Fotheringay in a pair of skin-tight jodhpurs at some horsey charity do my mother had organised.

I was going to get engaged on my nineteenth birthday, married on my twentieth. I was going to have four children—with a Norland nanny to do all the yucky stuff—breed prize-winning Irish setters and live happily ever after in a small Elizabethan manor house in Berkshire.

Perfect.

Unfortunately Peregrine Charles Fotheringay, a man of smouldering good looks and heir to the manor house in question, had had a career plan of his own. One that did not include me. At least, not in connection with the white lace, rings and marquee.

And when that plan fell apart I just hadn't had the heart to start again from scratch.

Probably because I didn't have a heart. I'd given it away. It was gathering dust somewhere, along with my career plan, in PCF's trophy cabinet.

My big mistake had been to believe, when he'd said he loved me, that marriage would follow. An even bigger mistake had been to fall totally, helplessly, hopelessly in love with him. I had discovered, too late, that men like him didn't marry for love, but for advantage. And, having taken full and frequent advantage of my stupidity—admittedly with my whole-hearted co-operation—he'd married the heiress to a fortune large enough to fund the expensive upkeep of the said Elizabethan manor and keep him in the kind of luxury to which he felt entitled. As his father had done before him, apparently.

As Perry had explained when I confronted him with a copy of *The Times* in which his name was linked with the said heiress under the heading 'Forthcoming Weddings', it was in the nature of a family business: Fotheringay men didn't work for their money; they married it.

The heiress was short-changed. For that kind of money she really should have got a title as well.

Anyway.

Here I was, spending my twenty-fifth birthday at an employment agency when I should have been organising a spur-of-the-moment frivolous celebratory bash for my friends. The kind that takes weeks to plan. I just hadn't got the heart. What was there to celebrate? I was twenty-five, for heaven's sake—that was a quarter of a century—and to make things worse my father had persuaded the trustees of my grandmother's trust fund to put a stop on my monthly allowance so that I would have to get a serious job and stand on my own two feet.

That would teach me to tell little white lies.

Three months ago, in a spectacularly successful attempt to toss my shy best friend into the path of a billionaire playboy, I'd made up a story about having to hang onto my job because my father was threatening to stop my allowance. Something he did on a fairly regular basis, but which we both knew was nothing but bluff and bluster.

But now he'd actually done it.

It was for my own good, he had assured me.

Oh, sure.

I might not be clever, like my sister Kate, but I wasn't stupid. I could see the way his mind was working. He thought that if I was short of money I'd have no choice but to return to the family nest and play housekeeper to him: a singularly unattractive prospect that offered all the undesirable aspects of marriage without any of the fun. Which was presumably why my mother had legged it with the first man to pay her a compliment since she'd walked down the aisle as Mrs Harrington.

'Well?'

Miss Frosty was getting impatient.

'Not a career plan as such,' I said. Even I could see that she wasn't going to be impressed with my romantic notions of connubial bliss. With the twenty-twenty vision of hindsight even I could see that it wasn't so much a career plan as total fantasy... 'I was never what you could describe as academic. My strengths are in what my mother described as "home skills".'

'Home skills?' She didn't actually get as far as smiling, but she did brighten considerably. 'What kind of home skills?'

'You know...flower arranging—that sort of stuff. I can do wonders with an armful of Rose Bay Willow Herb and Cow Parsley.'

'I see.' There was a significant pause. 'And do you have a City and Guilds qualification for this?' she asked finally. 'Something I can offer an employer as proof of your capabilities?'

I was forced to admit that I hadn't. 'But the Ladies' Home Union were jolly impressed when I stood in for my mother at the church flower festival at such short notice.' Well, they'd been polite anyway. No one had so much as breathed the word 'weeds'. Not within my hearing, anyway. Which, considering they'd been expecting the best blooms from my mother's garden, had been generous of them.

Unfortunately, when she'd decided she'd had enough of tweeds and dogs and jumble sales and departed for South Africa with the muscular professional from the golf club, my father had driven a tractor through her prize-winning roses. Then, when there was nothing left to flatten, he'd repeated this pointless act of vandalism by doing the same thing to her immaculate herbaceous borders.

Now, that *was* stupid. She wasn't there to have her heart broken over the destruction of all her hard work. She didn't even know he'd done it, for goodness' sake. And he was the one who had to live with the mess.

But after that Willow Herb and Cow Parsley had been all that I could lay my hands on in any quantity at such short notice.

'Anything else?'

'What? Oh...' I was beginning to get irritated by this woman. Just because I couldn't type a squillion words a minute, or do much more than send e-mails on my laptop, it didn't mean I was worthless.

Did it?

No. Of course not. There were all kinds of things I could do. And with a sudden rush of inspiration I said, 'I have organisational skills.'

I could organise great parties, for a start. That took skill. One look at Miss Frosty Face, however, warned me that party organising might not actually be considered much of an asset in the job market. Frivolity in the workplace was definitely a thing of the past.

But there were other things.

'I can organise a fundraiser for the Brownies, or a cricket club tea, or a church whist drive.' In theory, anyway. I'd never done any of those things single-handedly but, unlike my clever older sister, who had been too busy studying to get involved, I'd enjoyed helping my mother do all those things. It had been a heck of a lot more fun than revising for boring old exams, and it wasn't as if I'd had any intention of going to university. I'd been going to follow in my mother's footsteps—marry landed gentry and spend the rest of my life oiling the community wheels of village life.

Of course Kate had never had any trouble getting—or keeping—a job. And now she had a totally gorgeous barrister husband who adored her, too.

Maybe I should have paid more attention at school.

'I can produce fairy cakes in vast quantities, ditto scones and sandwiches at the drop of a hat.' I hadn't done it since I'd left home at eighteen—to avoid running into PCF in the village, driving his new Ferrari, a wedding present from his bride—but it was like riding a bicycle. Probably. 'And I can speak French, too,' I said, getting a bit carried away.

'Well?'

When I hesitated between lying through my teeth and a realistic appraisal of my linguistic skills she reeled off something double-quick in French. Too fast for me to understand, but I could tell it was a question because of the intonation. And I could make a good guess at what she was asking...

Show-off.

'And play the piano.' Before she could ask me the difference between a crotchet and a quaver I added, 'And I know how to address anyone, from a Duke to an Archbishop—'

'Then you appear to have missed your vocation,' she said, cutting me off before I made a total idiot of myself. Or maybe not. Her expression suggested that I was way beyond that point. 'You were clearly destined to marry one of the minor royals.'

I began to laugh. Too late I discovered I was on my own. This was not, apparently, her idea of a little light-hearted banter.

It occurred to me that this woman did not—unlike the much missed Peter—have a sense of humour. And, unlike him, she did not look upon a lack of formal qualifications as a challenge to her ingenuity; she just thought I was a total waste of space, a spoilt 'princess' who had some kind of nerve taking up her valuable time and expecting to be taken seriously.

It occurred to me, somewhat belatedly, that she might have a point, and that maybe I should consider a totally serious reappraisal of my entire life. And I would. Just as soon as I was in gainful employment.

'Look, I don't need a job that pays a fortune,' I told her. 'I just need to be able to pay the bills.' And treat myself to a new lipstick now and then. Not a fortune, but not exactly peanuts, either. At least I had the luxury of living rent-free, thanks to Aunt Cora, who preferred the guaranteed warmth of her villa in the south of France to the London apartment that had been part of her lucrative divorce settlement. I only hoped my mother had been taking notes... 'I'll consider anything. Really.'

'I see. Well, since your skills appear to be of the domestic variety, Miss Harrington, maybe you could put them to good use. I don't have much call for free-form flower arrangers just now, but how are you at cleaning?'

Cleaning? 'Cleaning what?'

'Anything that people will pay good money to someone else to clean for them rather than do it themselves. Cookers come top of the list, but kitchen floors and bathrooms are popular, too.'

She had got to be joking! The only cleaning fluid I'd handled recently came in small, expensive bottles from the cosmetic department at Claibourne & Farraday.

'I don't have any real experience in that direction,' I admitted.

Aunt Cora's flat came equipped with a lady who appeared three times a week and did anything that required the use of rubber gloves. She charged the earth on an hourly basis for her services, but I'd planned on sub-letting my sister's old room in order to pay her. And to cover some of the monthly maintenance charges. Just as soon as it was vacant. Unfortunately Aunt Cora had taken advantage of Kate's departure to offer her room to 'some very dear friends who need somewhere to stay in London while they're looking for a place of their own.'

I was hardly in a position to say that it wasn't convenient. Actually, at the time it had been fine, but that had been months ago and there was still no sign of them finding anywhere else. And, staying rent-free—

and, unlike me, expenses-free—in London, why would they be in any great hurry?

'Well, that's a pity. We can always find work for someone with the ability to apply themselves to a scrubbing brush. ' She gave a dismissive little shrug. 'But clearly that's an ''anything'' too far for you.' With that, Miss Frosty stood up to signal that as far as she was concerned the interview was over. But just to ram the point home she said, 'Should I be offered anything in your particular niche in the job market, I'll give you a call.'

She managed to make the prospect sound about as likely as a cold day in hell. That I could live with. It was the smirk she couldn't quite hide that brought an unexpectedly reckless 'I'll show her...' genie bubbling right out of the bottle.

'I said I was short of experience. I didn't say I wasn't prepared to give it a try.'

Even as I heard myself say the words I knew I'd regret it, but at least I had the satisfaction of surprising that look of superiority right off Miss Frosty's face. I hoped it would be sufficient comfort when I was on my knees with my head inside some bloke's greasy oven.

'Well, that's the spirit,' she said, finally managing a smile. It was a smug, self-satisfied little smile, and I had the strongest feeling that she couldn't wait to get stuck into the 'domestic' files and search for the nastiest, dirtiest job she could find. 'I've got your telephone number. I'll be in touch. Very soon.'

'Great,' I said, looking her straight in the eyes.

In the meantime I'd treat myself to the best pair of

rubber gloves money could buy. It was, after all, my birthday.

It would be fine, I told myself as I reached the pavement and, on automatic, raised my hand to hail a passing taxi. Then thought better of it and stood back to let someone else take it.

It would be fine. Peter would be back from his holiday in a week or two, he'd find me something to do, and life would return to normal—more or less. But in the meantime my expenses had doubled and my income had just become non-existent.

It wouldn't hurt to start economising and take a bus.

It wouldn't hurt to buy a newspaper and check out the job prospects for myself, either. The only possible excuse for not taking whatever revolting job Miss Frosty dug up for me—and I had no doubt that it would be revolting—would be that I was already gainfully employed.

The prospect of telling her so cheered me up considerably. It wasn't as if I was unemployable, or even lazy. I'd had *loads* of jobs. But the unappealing prospect of becoming unpaid housekeeper to my manipulative and thoroughly bad-tempered father was all the incentive I needed to stay seriously focussed. I was in the mood to show him, too.

Okay, so I'd majored in having fun for the last few years. I mean, what was there to be serious about? But I'd had a wake-up call, a reminder that I couldn't carry on like this indefinitely.

Apparently I was supposed to get serious now I'd turned twenty-five. Get a career plan.

Let's face it. I didn't even have a life plan.

It occurred to me that if I wasn't jolly careful another twenty-five years would drift by and I wouldn't have had a life.

Yes, it was definitely time to get serious.

I stopped at the corner shop to stock up on cat food, and while I was there picked up the evening paper. I scanned the ads while I was waiting for the girl behind the counter to stop flirting with a man buying a motorcycle magazine and discovered to my delight that I could job hunt on the internet, thus bypassing the doubtful pleasure of being made to feel totally useless on a face to face basis.

I also bought a notebook—one with a kitten on the cover and its own matching pen. I'd need a notebook if I was going to do all this planning. And, feeling virtuous, I circled all the likely job prospects in the paper while I was on the bus, jumping off at my stop fired up with enthusiasm and raring to go.

'*Big Issue*, miss?'

Saving money or not, I wasn't homeless like the man standing on this freezing corner selling copies of a magazine for a living.

'Hi, Paul. How's it going? Found anywhere to live yet?'

'It's looking good for after Christmas.'

'Great.' I handed over the money for the magazine and then bent down to make a fuss of the black and white mongrel pup sitting patiently at his side.

'Hello, boy.' He responded happily to a scratch behind the ear and I gave him a pound, too, which more or less cancelled out my economy with the taxi. 'Buy yourself a bone on me.'

I went in through the back entrance to the flats so that I could feed the little stripey cat who'd made a home there. She appeared at the first sound of kibble rattling in the dish. She was so predictable. Then I walked through to the lifts, grateful that my 'guests' were away for an entire week and determined to make a serious start on the job hunting front.

There were distractions waiting for me in the lobby, however.

I might be trying to ignore my birthday, but nobody else was taking the hint. The porter had a pile of cards for me, as well as a parcel from my sister—who was away visiting her in-laws for a family celebration—and some totally knockout flowers.

There was a whopping big bunch of sunflowers—my absolute favourite, and heaven alone knew where the florist had managed to get them this late in the year—from Ginny and Rich. I felt a lump forming in my throat. I was practically certain that it was a rule of being on honeymoon that you were supposed to be totally self-centred and forget that the rest of the world existed. I touched the bright petals. Not Ginny...

There was an orchid in a pot from Philly, too. I hadn't seen my here-today-gone-tomorrow next door neighbour in ages. She and Cal were always flitting off to some corner of a foreign field, or jungle, or mountain range to film exotic fauna. Neither of them had allowed the arrival of their baby daughter to slow them down, but just carried her along with them, papoose-style, wherever they went.

I'd have been okay if the arrangement of pale pink roses hadn't been from my mother.

I sniffed. Loudly. I refused to cry. I did not cry—I'd used up all the tears I was ever going to shed over Perry Fotheringay—but it was a close-run thing. Everyone in the world I loved was married, or away on an adventure, or busy getting a life. Not that I begrudged any of them one bit of happiness or success. I was just a little bit tired of endlessly playing the dizzy bridesmaid and doing my best to avoid catching the bouquet tossed so carefully in my direction before waving them off on their new lives. That was all.

I opened the package from my sister. Nestling inside the layers of tissue paper, I found a pot of industrial strength anti-wrinkle cream, support stockings and a pair of 'big knickers'. The card—'Over the hill? What hill? I didn't see any hill…'—that went with it contained a voucher for a day of total pampering with all the extras at a luxury spa. It was exactly what I needed.

A laugh and a bit of luxury.

I was still grinning when the phone began to ring. I picked it up, expecting to hear a raucous chorus of 'Happy Birthday to you' from one of the gang I hung around with.

'Sophie Harrington—single, sexy and celebrating—'

'Miss Harrington?' Miss Frosty's voice froze the smile on my face. 'How are you with dogs?'

'Dogs?'

She wanted me to wash dogs?

'One of our clients needs a dog-walker, and it occurred to me that this might be something you could do.'

Oh, very funny.

If this was her idea of 'changing my life' she could keep it. I'd go somewhere else. I cleared my throat, about to tell her what she could do with her dog-walking job; I just about managed to stop myself from saying it.

I'd said 'anything'. If this was a test I wasn't about to fail it just because I was too proud to walk some-one's dog for money. Not when I'd probably have done it for nothing, if asked nicely. Who was I kid-ding? Not *probably*—I'd have volunteered like a shot. I loved dogs. They were always the same. Up-front and honest. They had no hidden agendas, no secrets. They never let you down.

'How much an hour?' I asked. Since I hadn't been asked nicely, I might as well be businesslike about it.

She told me.

A dog-walker didn't rate as much per hour as a secretary, but if I was totally honest I had to admit that I could walk a lot better than I could type. And I couldn't afford to be choosy.

'Two hours a day—first thing in the morning and again in the evening,' she continued. 'It will leave you ample time to fit in other jobs during the day.'

'Great,' I said, the spectre of greasy ovens looming large. But it occurred to me that not only would I have a little money coming in—and I wasn't in any position to turn that down—I'd also have plenty of time to work on my career plan. Look for a proper job. 'When do I start?'

'This afternoon. It's a bit of a crisis situation.'

Naturally. Some idle bloke couldn't be bothered to walk his own dogs and it was a crisis.

'That's not a problem, is it?'

'Well, it is my birthday,' I replied sweetly. 'But I can take an hour out from the endless round of fun to walk a dog.'

'Two dogs.'

'Do I get paid per dog?' I asked. 'Or was the rate quoted for both of them?' I was learning 'business-like' fast.

'You're being paid for an hour of your time, Miss Harrington, not per dog.'

'So I'd be paid the same if I was walking one dog?'

I thought it was a fair question, but she didn't bother to answer. All she said was, 'The client's name is York. Gabriel York. If you've got a pen handy, I'll give you the address.'

I grabbed my new kitty notebook, with its matching pen, and wrote it down. Then, since the ability to put one foot in front of the other without falling over was the only potential of mine that Miss Frosty-Face was prepared to tap, I registered with a couple of online agencies who might ignore me but at least wouldn't be rude to my face.

CHAPTER TWO

I WAS late. It wasn't my fault, okay? People had kept phoning me to see what I was doing to celebrate my birthday. No one had believed me when I'd said nothing. They'd just laughed and said, 'No, really—what are you doing?' and in the end I'd relented and promised I'd meet Tony down the pub at nine o'clock.

Then my mother had phoned from South Africa, wanting to tell me about everything she'd been doing—well, obviously not *everything*—and I could hardly say I had more important things to do, could I?

Anyway, it was hardly a matter of life or death. Dogs couldn't tell the time and I didn't have to rush off anywhere else. They'd get their hour. Start twenty minutes late; finish twenty minutes late. Sorted.

Gabriel York's address proved to be a tall, elegant, terraced house in a quiet cul-de-sac untroubled by through traffic. Its glossy black front door was flanked by a pair of perfectly clipped bay trees which stood in reproduction Versailles boxes; no one in their right mind would leave the genuine lead antiques on their doorstep, even if it would take a crane to lift them. The brass door furniture had the well-worn look that only came from generations of domestics applying serious elbow grease—a fate, I reminded myself, that awaited me unless I gave some serious thought to my future.

The whole effect was just too depressingly perfect for words. Like something out of a costume drama, where no one was interested in the reality of the mud or the smell of nineteenth-century London.

This was a street made for designer chic and high, high heels, and I felt about as out of place as a lily on the proverbial dung heap.

My own fault, entirely.

I'd stupidly forgotten to ask what kind of dogs Mr York owned, and since there was no way I was going to call back and ask Miss Frosty to enlighten me I'd gone for the worst-case scenario, assuming something large and muscular, times two, and dressing accordingly. At home that would have meant one of the ancient waxed jackets that had been hanging in the mud room for as long as I could remember and a pair of equally venerable boots. The kind of clothes that my mother lived in.

Had lived in.

These days, as she'd told me at length, she was to be found stretched out poolside in a pair of shorts, a halter neck top and factor sixty sunblock. I didn't blame her; she was undoubtedly entitled to a bit of fun after a lifetime of waiting hand, foot and finger on my father for no reward other than an occasional grunt.

I just didn't want to be reminded of the difference between her life and my own, that was all.

Here in London it was doing something seasonal in the way of freezing drizzle, and although I'd stuffed my hair into a pull-on hat I hadn't been able to find a pair of gloves; my fingers were beginning to feel decidedly numb.

Anyway, without the luxury of a help-yourself selection of old clothes to choose from, I'd had to make do with my least favourite jeans, a faux-fur jacket—a worn-once fashion disaster that I'd been meaning to take to the nearest charity shop—and a pair of old shoes that my sister had overlooked when she moved out. They were a bit on the big side, but with the help of a pair of socks they'd do. They'd have to. I wasn't wearing my good boots to plough through the undergrowth of Battersea Park.

Now I realised that I looked a total mess for no good reason. I needn't even have bothered to change my shoes. I only had to take one look at those pompom bay trees to know that Mr York's dogs would be a couple of pampered, shaved miniature poodles, with pom-pom tails to match. They'd undoubtedly consider a brisk trot as far as Sloane Square a serious workout.

So, I asked myself as I mounted the steps to his glossy front door, what kind of man would live in a house like this? My imagination, given free reign, decided that Mr York would be sleek and exquisitely barbered, with small white hands. He'd have a tiny beard, wear a bow tie and do something important in 'the arts'. I admit to letting my prejudices run away with me here. I have a totally irrational dislike of clipped bay trees—and clipped poodles.

Poor things.

I rang the doorbell and waited to see just how well my imagination and reality coincided.

The dogs responded instantly to the doorbell—one with an excited bark, the other with a howl like a timber wolf in some old movie. One of them hurled itself at the door, hitting it with a thump so emphatic that it echoed distantly from the interior of the house and suggested I might have been a bit hasty in leaping to a judgement based on nothing more substantial than a prejudice against clipped bay trees.

If they were poodles they were the great big ones, with voices to match.

Unfortunately, the dogs were the only ones responding to the bell. The door remained firmly shut, with no human voice to command silence. No human footsteps to suggest that the door was about to be flung open.

Under normal circumstances I would have rung the bell a second time, but considering the racket the dogs were making my presence could hardly have gone unnoticed. So I waited.

And waited.

After a few moments the dog nearest the door stopped barking and the howl died down to a whimper, but apart from a scrabbling, scratching noise from the other side of the door as one of them tried to get at me that was it.

Seriously irritated—I wasn't *that* late and the dogs still needed to be walked—I raised my hand to the bell to ring again, but then drew back at the last minute, my outstretched fingers curling back into my palm as annoyance was replaced by a faint stirring of unease.

'Hello?' I said, feeling pretty stupid talking to a dog through a door. The scrabbling grew more anxious and I bent down, pushed open the letterbox and found myself peering into a pair of liquid brown eyes set below the expressive brows of a cream silky hound.

'Hello,' I repeated, with rather more enthusiasm. 'What's your name?'

He twitched his brows and whined sorrowfully.

Okay, I admit it was a stupid question.

'Is there anyone home besides you dogs?' I asked, trying to see past him into the hallway.

The intelligent creature backed away from the door, giving me a better look at his sleek short coat, feathery ears and slender body, then he gave a short bark and looked behind him, as if to say, 'Don't look at me, you fool, look over there…' And that was when I saw Gabriel York and realised I'd got it all wrong.

Twice over.

His dogs were not poodles and he wasn't some dapper little gallery owner in a bow tie.

Gabriel York was six foot plus of dark-haired, muscular male. And the reason he hadn't answered the door when I rang was because he was lying on the hall floor. Still. Unmoving.

I remembered the echoing thump. Had that been him, hitting the deck?

The second hound, lying at his side, lifted his head and looked at me for a long moment, before pushing his long nose against his master's chin with an anxious little whine, as if trying to wake him up. When that didn't have any effect he looked at me again, and the message he was sending came over loud and clear.

Do something!

Oh, crumbs. Yes. Absolutely. Right away.

I dug in my pocket, flipped open my cellphone and with shaking fingers punched in the number for the emergency services. I couldn't believe how much information they wanted—none of which I had. Apart from the address and the fact that I had an unconscious man on the other side of the door.

How did I know if he'd hit his head? And what difference would it make if I told them? It wasn't as if they could do anything about it until they got here…

Maybe I sounded a touch hysterical, because the woman in the control centre, in the same calming voice more commonly used to talk to skittish horses, over-excited dogs and total idiots, told me to stay right where I was. Someone would be with me directly.

The minute I hung up, of course, I realised that I should have told her the one thing I *did* know. That they wouldn't be able to get in. I looked around in the vain hope that a passing knight errant—and I'd have been quite happy to pass on the gleaming armour and white horse—might leap to my rescue and offer to pick the lock, or break a window, or do some other totally clever thing that had completely eluded me and climb in.

The street—and the way my day was going I was not surprised by this—was deserted.

Actually, on second thoughts, maybe that was just as well. I wasn't sure that anyone who could pick a lock at the drop of a hat would be a knight errant. Not unless he was a bona fide locksmith, anyway.

I looked through the letterbox again, hoping, in the way that you do, that Gabriel York had miraculously recovered while I'd been panicking on his doorstep.

There was no discernible change. Was he actually breathing?

'Mr York?' It came out as little more than a whisper. 'Mr York!' I repeated more sharply.

The only response was from the dogs, who reprised the bark/howl chorus, presumably in the hope of rousing someone more useful.

Oh, help! I had to do *something*. But what? I didn't have any hairpins about my person, and even if I had I couldn't pick a lock to save my life. His life.

I looked over the railing down into the semi-basement. The only window down there was not just shut, it had security bars, too, so breaking it wouldn't be much use.

I took a step back and looked up at the house. The ground-floor windows were all firmly fastened, but, blinking the drizzle out of my eyes, I could see that one of the sash cord windows on the floor above street level was open just a crack. It wasn't that far, and there was a useful downpipe within easy reach. Well, easyish reach, anyway.

I stowed my phone and, catching hold of the iron railing that guarded the steps, pulled myself up. Then, from the vantage point of this precious perch, I grabbed the downpipe and hitched myself up until I was clinging, monkey-like, with my hands and feet. I didn't pause to gather my breath. I was very much afraid that if I paused to do *anything* I'd lose my nerve. Instead I clung with my knees, reached up with my hands, pushed with my feet. The cast iron was cold, damp and slippery—and a lot harder to climb than I'd anticipated.

I hadn't got very far when the muscles in my upper

arms began to burn, reminding me that I hadn't been to the gym in a while. Actually, I really should make the most of it before my membership expired, I thought, and slipped, banging my chin and biting my lip in the process.

Concentrate, you silly cow...

Quite. I gritted my teeth and, telling myself not to be such a wimp, hauled myself up. Things didn't improve when I finally got level with the window, which was rather further from the pipe than it had looked from the ground. Just a bit more of a stretch. Excellent from a security point of view, but an unnervingly sickening distance to span from mine.

It was perhaps fortunate that the biggest spider I'd ever seen decided to investigate the bipedal blundering that had disturbed whatever it was that spiders do when they lurk behind downpipes—and frankly I'd rather not know—thus confirming the fact that I would rather risk the fall into a stone basement area than endure a face-to-face encounter with eight horribly long though undoubtedly harmless legs.

Idiotic, no doubt, but as a force for overcoming inertia arachnophobia takes some beating.

Have you ever wished you hadn't started something? Just wished you'd never got out of bed that morning?

It was my birthday. I was twenty-five years old and everyone was telling me that it was time to grow up. As if I hadn't done that the day I'd realised that love was no competition for money.

But, clinging to Gabriel York's windowsill by my fingernails, I had a moment of truth. Reality. Let me live through this, I promised whatever unfortunate deity had been given the task of looking after total idiots, and I will embrace maturity. I'll even get to grips with my dislike of technology and sign up for a computer course.

In the meantime I dug in and hauled myself up, trying not to think about my expensive manicure—probably the last one I'd ever be able to afford—as my nails grated against stone and, with my knee on the sill, I managed to grab hold of the window and push it upwards.

Someone must have been listening to my plea for help because, unlike the sash cord windows of my family home, which stuck like glue in damp weather, Mr York kept his well oiled and perfectly balanced. In response to a shove with the full force of my bodyweight behind it the window shot up and I fell in, landing in a painful heap on a polished oak floor, closely followed by a spindly table and something fragile that shattered noisily very close to my ear.

Make that half listening. Bumped chin, bitten lip, wrecked nails, and now I had a throbbing shoulder to add to the tally. And my knees hurt. This job definitely came under the heading 'life-changing'. Whether I'd survive it was yet to be proved.

I opened my eyes and was confronted by the ruin of what might have been a Dresden shepherdess. And something told me that this wasn't a replica. It was the real thing.

I blamed its total destruction on the latest craze for ripping up carpets and polishing original wooden floors. If there had been a draught-stopping fitted carpet, with a thick cushion underlay, the shepherdess would have still been in one piece and I wouldn't have bruised my knees. And, of the two, it was my knees I was more bothered about. The shepherdess would undoubtedly be insured for replacement value. My knees were unique.

Not that I had any time to lie there and feel sorry for myself. Somewhere in the distance I could hear the sound of a siren—hopefully that of the ambulance I'd summoned. I had to get to the front door and let in the paramedics…

I got up and pulled down the window, leaving grubby fingermarks. I rubbed my hands down the front of my jeans before I left them on anything else, and headed for the door. Not before noting that the room, like the Dresden shepherdess, did not quite fit the glimpse I'd got of Gabriel York. It was a thoroughly feminine room. Presumably the territory of Mrs York. I blamed her for the bay trees while I was at it.

And where was she when her husband needed her to walk his dogs? Pick him up off the floor? Call an ambulance…?

The nearest dog—clearly an adolescent—leapt on me in his excitement as I ran down the stairs, nearly knocking me off my feet again.

'Get off, you stupid hound,' I said, pushing him away, trying not to look too closely at my employer as I stepped over him—if he'd fallen downstairs and broken his neck I'd rather not know—and went to open the door.

I looked out. No ambulance… Well, it was building up to the rush hour, so it would undoubtedly have to battle its way through the traffic, like the rest of London.

It was down to me, then. I left the door ajar, so that they could get in when they arrived, and turned back to face the man who lay supine and unmoving, taking up most of the floor.

And I got a reprise of the 'do something' look from the dog lying protectively at his side.

Deep breath, Sophie. You can do this...

'Mr York...' I knelt down beside him and it didn't take a genius to see that even when he was on his feet Gabriel York wasn't going to look terribly well. His skin had a yellowish pallor and his face was drawn-out and haggard with the sharply attenuated features of someone who's lost a great deal of weight without any of the tiresome bother of going on a diet. He was wearing a black dressing gown over a pair of cotton pyjama pants—which, considering it was late afternoon, suggested that it wasn't simply idleness that had stopped him from walking his dogs.

He might, of course, have slipped on the stairs— his feet were bare—as he'd come down to answer the door. Or one of the dogs might have got underfoot in its excitement and unbalanced him.

But, looking at him, I would have gambled that he'd just passed out. At least I hoped that was all he'd done; I gingerly touched his throat, seeking a pulse.

I couldn't find one.

The hound who'd been guarding him, but who had shifted slightly to let me get closer, licked my hand encouragingly. I patted him absently, swallowing as I attempted to dislodge a great big rock that suddenly seemed to be stuck in my throat.

How long had he been lying there? Was it too late for the kiss of life?

How long had it been since I'd rung the bell and heard that distant thump that I was now certain had been Gabriel York hitting the floor? He was still warm to the touch, but then my own hands were freezing. I rubbed them together, trying to get the feeling back into them.

I'd never actually given anyone the kiss the life, but I'd seen a demonstration once, years ago in the village hall, at a first aid course organised by my mother. You covered the victim's mouth and blew. No, there was more to it than that. Think, think... I put my hand beneath his neck and tilted it back to clear the airway. I remembered that much.

As I looked down into his face, forcing myself to take steady, even breaths—I hadn't realised until then that my heart was beating rather too fast for comfort—it occurred to me that even in extremis Gabriel York had an austere beauty, that his wide, sensual mouth was the kind a girl might enjoy kissing under less trying circumstances. At least she would if she was into kissing and all the messy stuff that inevitably followed.

Heartbreak, pain...

I forced myself to concentrate, cupping his chin in my hand and placing my lips over his to seal off the air.

His unshaven chin was bristly against my palm, my fingers. His mouth was cool, but not cold...

I forced myself to concentrate and blew steadily into his mouth.

At this point I nearly passed out myself from lack

of oxygen. I'd been concentrating so hard on remembering what to do that I'd missed out the vital step of taking a breath first. Okay. I'd got it now. Breath in, mouth to mouth, blow. And again.

How long was I supposed to keep this up? As if in answer, I heard that long-ago demonstrator sternly warning that once you began CPR you had to continue until relieved…

How much longer was the ambulance going to be?

I paused for another breath, and this time when I looked at him he seemed to have regained a little colour. Encouraged, I tried again.

There was a definite change—the kind of response that if I didn't know better would have given me the distinct impression that I was being—well, kissed back. No, definitely kissed back…

Oh, sugar…

I opened my eyes—that level of concentration had required my eyes to be tightly shut—and discovered that I was not imagining things. Clearly I had this kiss of life thing down to a fine art, because Gabriel York had his eyes open, too. Black, glittering behind quite scandalously thick lashes, and dangerously over-heated. Quite suddenly, I was the one in need of mouth-to-mouth resuscitation.

Rapidly recovering my wits—I had a highly developed sense of self-preservation where thick dark lashes were concerned—I decided it was time to put a safe distance between us. He was having none of that; his arm was around my waist before the message from my brain reached my limbs, holding me with rather more strength than anyone who'd been unconscious just moments before should have been able to summon up.

'Who the devil are you?' he demanded.

Huh? Whatever happened to, Thank you for saving my life?

Charitably putting his brusqueness down to disorientation—and bearing in mind that my electricity bill was in his hands—I didn't say the first thing that leapt into my mind. Instead I replied—somewhat breathlessly, it's true—'I'm Sophie Harrington.' All my spare breath had been pumping up his lungs, okay? I would have offered him my hand at this point, and said the obligatory How d'you do?, but one of my hands was already busy cradling his chin, while the other was doing something Florence Nightingale-ish in the vicinity of his brow. I immediately stopped that nonsense and, in the absence of any other bright conversation ideas, said, 'I've sent for an ambulance. It should be here any minute.'

'What the hell did you do that for?' he demanded, with a lack of gratitude that I found just a bit galling, considering all I'd been through.

'Because you were unconscious—'

'Rubbish!'

'You had your eyes closed, you didn't respond to the doorbell and…and I couldn't find a pulse.'

'Where did you look?' I stopped cradling his chin and pressed my fingers against his Adam's apple. He moved my hand to the right and pushed it firmly beneath his chin. 'Try there.'

'Oh…' He definitely had a pulse. His heart was beating almost as fast as mine.

He made a move to sit up, but, hoping to retrieve

some credibility in the first aid department, I said,
'Look, you were out cold. I think you should roll over
into the recovery position and wait for the paramedics.' He made no attempt to obey instructions and he
was too big for me to push him—at least he was if
he didn't want to be pushed—so I said, 'In your own
time.'

I added a smile, just so he'd know he was in safe
hands.

All I got for my pains was a scowl, but at least he
was alive and talking. Whether he was quite making
sense only time would tell. Whatever. I'd done my
bit, and at this point I should have been safe in assuming that nothing worse could happen. Indeed, that
when he'd recovered sufficiently to realise that I'd
risked my life to save his he would be transformed
into Mr Congeniality and I would be showered with
thanks for bravery above and beyond the call of dog-
walking duties. Possibly. I could wait.

Instead, still frowning, he said, 'Why were you
kissing me?' From his tone, I didn't get the impression it was an experience he would wish to repeat any
time soon.

Well, snap.

'I wasn't kissing you,' I replied, losing the smile.
What did he think I was? Some crazy woman who
leapt on unconscious men? I wanted to make sure he
understood that I did not kiss men I didn't know, and
even if I did I certainly wouldn't have to wait until
they were unconscious. 'I was giving you the kiss of
life.'

He barked out something that might have been a
laugh. The dismissive kind that lacked any kind of

humour or warmth. 'That had about as much in common with CPR as—'

I was spared whatever unflattering comparison he had in mind as a couple of uniformed policemen, taking advantage of the fact that I'd left the door ajar for the paramedics, burst into the hall. One of them grabbed me by the arm and without so much as a by-your-leave hauled me to my feet with an, 'All right, young lady…'

With that, pandemonium broke out as the older of the two dogs—the one that had been keeping watch over Gabriel York—leapt up, pushing himself between me and the policemen. From somewhere deep in his throat he produced a low, threatening growl that he might well have learned from his master.

The other dog immediately stopped dancing excitedly about the new arrivals and joined in. My heroes.

'Percy! Joe! Down.'

Percy, still baring his teeth but lowering the growl until it was scarcely audible, obeyed his master's voice in his own good time, his haunches almost but not quite in contact with the floor, ready to spring to my defence at the slightest provocation. Joe followed his example. The policeman, taking heed of this canine warning that any injudicious move would be met with extreme prejudice, let go of my arm and took a step back.

'Would someone like to tell me what the hell is going on?'

Gabriel York had taken advantage of the distraction to sit up and now, grabbing hold of the stairpost, he hauled himself to his feet.

'No…' I began. He glared at me for apparently

daring to defy him. More gently, I said, 'You really should sit down, Mr York.'

He gave me a look that suggested he would deal with me later, before ignoring my advice and turning to the nearest policeman. 'You,' he said. 'What are you doing here?'

'One of your neighbours called us, sir. She saw this young woman—' he unwisely gestured in my direction, got a warning reprise of the growl from Percy for his trouble and immediately lowered his arm '—er, apparently breaking in through an upstairs window and called the local station.'

Gabriel York turned back to look at me. Sweat had broken out on his upper lip and he looked as if he was about to pass out again at any minute. But not, apparently, before he'd got some answers. 'Is that right? You climbed in through an upstairs window?'

'I had to do something!' I was absolutely livid. I'd been out there, hanging on by my fingernails, risking my life, and instead of coming to help me his nosy neighbour had sat behind her curtains and called the police. Actually, my own legs felt suddenly less than solid as I had a quick flashback of the risks I'd taken. 'I couldn't just leave you lying there.'

'How did you know I was—' he made a gesture in the direction of the floor '—lying there?'

'Look, my name is Sophie Harrington,' I said, turning to the nearest policeman. 'I was sent here by the Garland Agency. They'll vouch for me. When no one answered the doorbell I looked through the letterbox and saw Mr York lying unconscious—' he snorted dismissively at this '—lying unconscious,' I repeated, 'on the floor at the foot of the stairs, so I climbed up the downpipe and in through the window.'

The policeman turned to Gabriel York for a response to this. This time he didn't snort. After a few moments' silent contemplation he nodded, then winced, then said, 'My neighbour undoubtedly did the correct thing, but Miss Harrington is right—' well, hallelujah '—she's here to walk my dogs.'

'Lifesaving is all part of the service,' I volunteered, earning myself another black look.

'I'm sorry you've been bothered, gentlemen,' he added, clearly hoping they'd leave so that he could collapse quietly. To be honest, he looked so grim that I had to force myself to stay put and not rush over to him and make him sit down before he collapsed in a heap at the foot of the stairs. Something warned me that it would not be a good idea.

Fortunately I did have one ace up my sleeve. I turned to the policemen. 'They're not the only ones who've been bothered, I'm afraid. Before I climbed in through the upstairs window and applied the kiss of life—'

'I was not dead!'

No. He certainly wasn't that. Even in extremis he'd managed a fairly good impression of being very much alive.

'—I called for an ambulance,' I finished, as if I had not been interrupted, hoping that I sounded as if I didn't care one way or another if it ever arrived.

'Then you can ring them again and call them off.'

The effort of talking was exhausting him, but his eyes held mine with an inner power. They were full of anger at his own weakness, hating me for having seen him that way, and I knew that there was no way I was going to be keeping this job—which was, I suppose, why I shrugged and said, 'If you can make it to the phone, Mr York, you can call them off your-self. Otherwise you're stuck with them.' I smiled at the younger of the two policemen. He looked barely old enough to shave. Blissfully, he blushed. 'You'll stay until the paramedics arrive, gentlemen? These poor dogs really have to do what a dog has to do.'

They raised no objection.

The dogs' leads were looped over a chair, along with—oh, joy—a pooper-scooper and some plastic bags. I picked them up, fastened the leads to the dogs' collars and, leaving my employer in the capable care of two strapping policemen, said, 'Okay, boys. Walkies.'

Joe needed no second bidding, leaping to his paws, his feathered tail whirling, his slender cream body quivering with excitement beneath his short silky coat. Percy looked to his master.

Gabriel York never took his eyes off me, and I found myself reliving the moment when the kiss of life had become something much more personal, re-membering exactly how his lips had felt beneath mine, how his dark hair had felt beneath my hand as I'd brushed it back from his forehead. The strength of his jaw as I'd cradled it…

Then, with the slightest movement of his hand, he gave his dogs permission to go, and with a jerk on my aching shoulder I found myself being towed through the door, down the steps and into the street.

An ambulance turned the corner as we headed in the direction of Battersea Park and I grinned.

Obviously he hadn't got to the phone in time.

It was only when I reached the park and set the dogs loose that I wondered what on earth I was going to do with them if the paramedics carted him off to hospital.

CHAPTER THREE

THE alarm was like a chainsaw chewing through my brain. That was the trouble with surprise parties. They took you by surprise and you didn't have time to remind yourself of the golden rule about not drinking on an empty stomach. More particularly the platinum, diamond-encrusted rule about not drinking too many margaritas on an empty stomach.

Since I'd been expecting nothing more than a quiet drink with a mate, I hadn't made a huge effort with my appearance either, going for comfort rather than glamour. I'd taken a long hot shower, to remove what seemed like half of Battersea Park, filed down the ruins of my nails and decided to forgo the doubtful pleasure of spending hours with a brush and hairdryer in an effort to return my hair to sleek perfection, and gone for the rumpled, dragged-through-a-hedge-backwards look instead.

Well, it had come close.

A dab of concealer on the nicely developing bruise, a pair of favourite—if past their fashion statement days—trousers, a baggy shirt and a pair of boots and I'd been all set.

Then I'd walked into the bar.

Everyone else had been dressed to kill, of course. I'd been the only one actually in the mood to perform the deed.

Tony, a bloke a girl could usually rely on not to

do anything clever, had ignored my 'I do not want to even think about this birthday, let alone celebrate it' response to his query about a party. He'd assumed that I was joking—I said he wasn't clever—and pulled out all the stops.

But—and these are probably the three most damning words in the English language—he'd meant well. To be honest, after the second margarita what I was wearing hadn't seemed to matter that much, and I'd surprised myself by having a great time. Cleverer than I thought, perhaps…

I groped for the clock, turned it off and fell out of bed while I was still awake. A walk—a long walk with two very lively dogs—would undoubtedly be good for me. Always assuming I could remember how to put one foot in front of another. Always assuming I still had a job.

On my return to Gabriel York's house yesterday I had been met by a frosty-faced Mrs York, who had wordlessly handed me a large towel at arm's length and watched from a safe distance while I'd removed all traces of mud from the dogs. Then, with the minimum of words, she'd indicated I should take them downstairs to the utility room and give them some water. After I'd removed my shoes. Clearly she didn't 'do' dogs.

Actually, I sympathised. She'd been wearing a charcoal grey business suit that had clearly cost a mint and in her place I wouldn't have wanted two excitable and muddy hounds near me. Honesty compels me to admit that it had been a mistake not to clip their leads back on before we reached the lake. It was asking for trouble and, as usual, I got it. They'd instantly spotted a couple of ducks so far away that I hadn't noticed them and plunged right in, proving to be selectively deaf when I'd called them to heel.

They'd heard 'walkies', no problem.

Anyway, I'd mopped up the resulting mess under her chilling gaze, and in an effort to break the ice— and because I had a stake in his health, besides really wanting to know—enquired after Mr York. All the time I'd been out with the dogs I'd wondered whether he'd been hauled off in an ambulance, undoubtedly protesting that it wasn't in the least bit necessary, and what I was going to do if he had.

No worries. There'd been lights on all over the place when I returned. Great. And Mrs York was there to answer the door. Not so great.

In reply to my query, she had informed me that he was 'as well as could be expected under the circumstances'—which told me precisely nothing. I mean, I'd have liked to know if he was suffering from a bad bout of something flulike so that I could stock up on painkillers and tissues. One look at her had suggested it might not be advisable to explain about my 'kiss of life'. She hadn't looked as if she'd appreciate my sacrifice.

What she had done, was leave me with the unsettling impression that the 'circumstances' had everything to do with me.

Tempted as I'd been to point out that I'd actually saved his life—probably—I had restrained myself. A fair number of silky cream dog hairs, disturbed by my brisk towelling of Joe's coat, had floated in her direction and attached themselves to her skirt; I hadn't wanted to be around when she noticed them.

She hadn't mentioned the shattered figurine in her sitting room. It had occurred to me, however, that it could be the reason for the below-zero welcome. I have to say that I wouldn't be in the least bit surprised if she and Miss Frosty-Face were closely related. It was hardly any wonder that Gabriel York was such a grouch.

I had half expected to find a message from my least favourite job-finder on the answering machine when I got home, informing me smugly that I'd failed at even this undemanding task and my services were no longer required.

No message. Maybe dog-walkers were in short supply. Maybe I could name my own price. More likely she'd known she wouldn't be able to get anyone else to take my place by eight o'clock the next morning and I'd simply been granted a temporary reprieve until she found a more competent replacement.

It occurred to me that once I'd taken Gabriel York's dogs for a run I'd be well advised to check my e-mail and see if the internet employment agency I'd contacted had lived up to its promise and sent me a load of jobs that would suit me perfectly. Since that seemed unlikely, I'd also follow up a number of possibilities I'd circled in the newspaper. The 'working from home' one hadn't mentioned computers...

I used industrial quantities of one of those wake-you-up shower gels on my unwilling limbs, reminding myself that in the meantime the dog-walking would just about keep the wolf from the door. Today, I told the brown stripey cat as I went out, I would be on time if it killed me.

She was sympathetic, rubbing against my legs as I

gave her a handful of kibbles while keeping an eye out for the porter, who strongly disapproved of me giving her any encouragement to stay. I would have taken her in if pets were allowed at Chandler's Reach. No cats. No dogs. Nothing that couldn't be safely confined to a cage.

My experience with the little white lie about my allowance should really have taught me not to tempt fate.

Okay, so the journey to work hadn't killed me. I'd arrived on Gabriel York's doorstep in one piece, but it was no thanks to London Underground. The escalator hadn't been working when I arrived at my stop and I'd had two choices. Wait for it to be fixed or walk up to street level.

It was about a million steps, and whilst any other day I would have breezed the climb, my over-indulgence in margaritas meant that I'd arrived at street level dry-mouthed, panting and gasping for water.

By the time I'd queued at the kiosk, bought a bottle, swallowed enough of the stuff to ensure that I'd live and was once again bracketed by the mop-head bay trees, I was—and you will already have guessed this—late again.

It was as if some dark force didn't want me to have this job, and to be brutally frank I wasn't that keen on ringing the doorbell. Nothing good had come from it yet. Putting if off wasn't likely to improve matters, though. But, whatever happened in the next few minutes, I vowed that I would not be climbing up that downpipe again.

Having cheered myself up with that promise, I finally rang the bell. Somewhere a long way off I heard Percy and Joe barking in joyous expectation and the cheering up process was complete. It was, I decided, highly probable that I liked dogs better than I did people. Some people anyway.

Then Gabriel York, scowling for the Olympics, opened the door. And I knew I did.

I hadn't, even when over-indulging in the party spirit, quite been able to get him out of my mind. I kept recalling that moment when I opened my eyes and saw him looking at me. And the moment when my attempt at mouth-to-mouth resuscitation had become something else…

If I hadn't already been rather pink in the face from my exertions, I might have blushed.

Totally ridiculous.

Actually, he did look marginally better than he had moments before I'd been dragged through the door by his hounds. He'd shaved, and he was dressed in well-worn grey sweats—the kind you pull on when your skin can't stand the chafing of anything more demanding—but it occurred to me that he didn't go with the bay trees. Unlike his designer-perfect wife.

'Miss Harrington,' he said wearily. 'Are you always half an hour late for work? Or are you just doing your best to kill me?'

'Definitely trying to kill you,' I replied. I could do sarcasm without any prompting from him, but it always helped to have someone worthy of one's best efforts. You'll have worked out for yourself by this time that I was my own worst enemy. Then, because he was leaning rather heavily on the door for support—and as if I hadn't tempted providence enough for one day—I added, 'Should you be out of bed?'

'Not according to anyone with an opinion on the matter,' he conceded, apparently caught offside by my counter-attack. This didn't look like a man who was used to admitting he was wrong—ever. About anything. He stood back to let me inside without bothering to check my footwear for mud. 'But since I'd just about given up on you I didn't seem to have a choice.'

'And?' I prompted, wiping my feet really thoroughly. I thought he had enough problems without me leaving muddy footprints all over the hall floor.

'I'm sorry?'

I had the distinct feeling they weren't two words he used often—at least not as an apology. Along with those other special words—thank you. For risking life and limb to save his. Life.

But then he wasn't apologising. He was simply prompting me to elaborate.

'Are you telling me that you've risen from your bed of pain to take Percy and Joe for a nice long rootle around the park yourself?' I enquired, sweetness itself. Clearly Mrs York wasn't going to do it for him. Where was his wife anyway? He shouldn't be left on his own. He should be tucked up in bed with someone to bring him warm drinks and hot water bottles and home-made chicken soup.

My smart mouth earned me another scowl, probably—no, definitely—deserved. Even if I was not to blame I was still horribly late.

'Regrettably not. If I was capable of walking anywhere further than the bathroom I wouldn't need you.'

He was frank, too.

'I was going to let them out into my sister-in-law's immaculate garden and earn myself two black marks. Not that she deserves any better.'

She was his sister-in-law? Not his wife? My heart leapt in the most ridiculous manner. This man was favourite for the Grouch of the Month award, for heaven's sake. Maybe of the year. Why would my heart be interested?

'Two black marks?'

'One for getting up and slowing down my recovery, thus prolonging my imposition on her busy life. One for letting the dogs do—'

'Right,' I said. I'd got the picture.

She wasn't his wife, and she not only disliked his dogs she didn't much care for him, either.

And? What possible interest was that to me?

He sketched a shrug. 'I would, of course, have blamed you.' The thought appeared to cheer him slightly. '*Are* you always late?' he repeated.

'Certainly not.' I was outraged at the suggestion. No matter how near the truth it might be. 'I started out in plenty of time—' as indeed I had; it was simply that events had conspired against me '—unfortunately there was a problem on the—'

He held up his hand to stop me. It was a big, square hand, with long, sexy fingers, attached to a thick wrist, a strong arm...

Maybe I was staring at it rather too obviously—hands are so important in a man—because somewhat self-consciously he clenched it into a fist, then dropped it back to his side. 'Spare me the details,' he said. I was clearly wearing what little patience he possessed so thin that it was practically transparent. 'I just thought that if it was standard I'd book you for half an hour earlier in the hope that you might arrive before Percy and Joe had chewed the door off the utility room in desperation.'

The corners of his eyes crinkled promisingly in what might have been the beginning of a smile before he remembered that he was being irritable and thought better of it. I didn't care. He wasn't going to phone Miss Frosty-Face and ask for a replacement!

Quite suddenly I wanted to hug him. Well, not that suddenly, really. The thought had been there all the time, just looking for an excuse—just as an experiment. To see if yesterday's surprising response was a one-off.

I mean, for heaven's sake, he'd looked as if he was at death's door. Hardly love's young dream. But then I'd already tried that with PCF.

Remembering him made it so much easier to restrain myself.

I wasn't in the market for dreams of any kind. But especially not the romantic variety.

'Really, it isn't necessary,' I said, doing a rather good job of keeping the desire to grin from breaking out all over my face, too. My job was apparently safe, but this was just two hours a day walking dogs, not personal assistant to some movie star. Or anyone the slightest bit interesting who didn't expect me to be clever with computers. 'I may be reduced to dog-walking to earn a living, but I can tell the time,' I said, perhaps a little more briskly than was entirely justified. I was late for the second day running. And I'd only been doing the job for two days. Then, 'Maybe I should get started,' I said. 'Joe and Percy are beginning to sound hysterical.'

'After yesterday they've been confined to the utility room,' he said, and with that any chance of a smile receded into the far distance. 'It's downstairs. Take them out through the rear—there's a gate leading to the mews at the back.' He reached out and took my hand, placed a key, warm from his pocket, into my palm, and then closed my fingers about it, holding them closed for a moment. 'It's kept locked.' And this time his dark eyes did warm, momentarily. 'To keep out burglars.'

An hour with Percy and Joe was a spirit-lifting adventure. They were so overjoyed to be free that it was impossible not to respond to their excitement as they rootled through the woods, exploring all the wildest bits of the park before doing a reprise of their duck-hunting in the lake.

They moved like greased lightning, and Percy returned with the tail feathers of a mallard, fat and lazy from the easy living in a London park, clenched between his teeth. These dogs were clearly bred to hunt rather than live in designer chic in Belgravia. They needed space and should be living out in the country.

Under other circumstances I might have volunteered to take them home. That was dog paradise. No one there had ever made a fuss about scuff marks on the doors or mud on the carpet.

My mother, when she'd phoned, hadn't enquired about the man she'd been married to for best part of thirty years. But she had asked about her old spaniel. He was getting on, poor love, and would be missing her dreadfully.

I blinked, surprised by a tear.

I totally lost track of time, but, mud-splattered and happy, we eventually arrived back at the York homestead.

The happiness did not last.

Gabriel York met me at the back door with a face that would curdle milk. 'Where the hell have you been?' he demanded. 'I thought you'd—'

'What? Lost them?'

He drew in a sharp, annoyed breath—whether he was annoyed with himself or with me I couldn't say—dragged his fingers distractedly through his thick dark hair and said, 'You're back in one piece; that's all that matters. But if they're too much for you to handle—'

'No. I'm sorry if you were worried, but we were just having too much fun to stop. Although to be honest—' I dug around in my pocket, found the duck feathers and put them on the nearest work surface '—I'm not too sure about the legal position on duck-hunting in London parks. This one got away, but it was a near thing. I rely on you to bail me out if necessary. What kind of dogs are they?'

'Salukis. Persian greyhounds. They're sight-hunters. I'm sorry, I should have warned you that they'll see stuff long before you do.'

'You weren't in much of a state to do anything that useful,' I reminded him. 'You still look pretty ropey, actually. If you don't mind me saying.' Ignoring the way his mouth tightened as he resisted the urge to tell me that he minded very much, I said, 'I'll bring you a cup of tea when I've rubbed these two down.'

'You will?' He looked as if he really didn't want to ask the next question. But he just couldn't help himself. 'Where will I be?'

'Lying down.' He really did look out on his feet, gaunt and a bit grey around the mouth, and whilst I had no serious objection to giving him the kiss of life again I didn't want to seem too eager; he might get the wrong idea. Or maybe it was the right one; much worse. 'In bed. Before you fall down,' I added, in my bossiest nanny-type voice. It hadn't worked on the dogs, but I had an ace up my sleeve. 'I warn you, Mr York, if I have to call an ambulance again I'll stay and make sure they take you away in it this time.'

'Do that,' he warned, 'and the dogs will have to go into boarding kennels. And you'll be out of a job.'

'No!'

'Cristabel is only putting up with them because she thinks having them around is good for me,' he replied. 'She's only putting up with me because I was released from hospital on the sole understanding that I was not going to be on my own.' He shrugged. 'As you've noticed, I get dizzy spells.'

'Is that what you're calling it? I'd have said you passed out cold, myself.' Which was rather unkind since, gratifyingly, he hadn't mistaken my horror for selfishness but concern on behalf of the dogs.

'She's really being very generous,' he continued, ignoring my interruption, 'but I suspect that broken figurine in her sitting room is trying her patience practically beyond endurance.'

Oh, right. Ace up sleeve fielded and neatly returned.

'That wasn't the dogs,' I said, owning up. 'But you already know that...'

Creases at the corners of his eyes fanned unexpectedly into a wry smile. 'I know that. The dogs know that. But I've given her a hard enough time already without putting her in the position of having to explain to her insurance company how easily you managed to climb in through an upstairs window—'

'It wasn't *easy*. I've got the broken fingernails to prove it.' I displayed them for his inspection and, quite unexpectedly, he took my hands, holding them as he looked at the shortened version of what had only yesterday been long, well-manicured perfection. Then, after what seemed liked hours, a sudden tremor seized him and he dropped them.

'Even so,' he said, abruptly, 'a burglar wouldn't have worried about his nails, and I suspect they'd take exception to the lack of security and raise her premiums.'

'It's fortunate the window was open. A piece of china can be replaced—'

'Possibly,' he snapped, before I could suggest that he couldn't be. He stuffed his hands into his pants pockets and lost the smile. 'But she'd still blame the dogs. If they hadn't been here you wouldn't have had to climb in through the window.'

'Someone should have been here to let me in.'

'If you'd been on time my brother would have been. He was supposed to walk them himself, but there's been some sort of crisis...' He stopped, shrugged. 'He waited for as long as he could. I'd just about given up on you and was on my way down to let them out into the garden.'

Oh, knickers. That was what he'd meant by me trying to kill him. He should have been in bed last night. And undoubtedly I'd messed up the system again this morning. And then I'd spent ages longer than my allocated hour in the park.

He should be there right now. Which made me feel bad. But one thing was clear: he wasn't staying in this horrible house out of choice. And that cheered me up enormously. Ridiculous, but there it was. Not that he seemed to be getting too much in the way of TLC from his busy family. Considering he wasn't supposed to be left on his own.

I kept the questions to myself and said, 'In that case I suggest you go back to bed, Mr York, before you collapse and the situation is taken out of both our hands.'

'Gabriel,' he said. 'Or Gabe, if you find that a bit of a mouthful.'

'Gabriel is fine,' I said, without having to think about it. 'I'm Sophie. If you ever call me Soph you'll be walking your own dogs.'

'Sophie.' He regarded me steadily for a long moment. 'I won't forget.'

'Good. And I'll make an effort to be on time in future.' How, I wasn't sure, but I'd think of something. 'Just go back to bed, Gabriel.'

It felt oddly intimate—exchanging names, ordering him to bed as if I'd known him for ever instead of being total strangers. Feeling unexpectedly self-conscious, I busied myself getting out of the hideous faux-fur, pulled off the close-fitting hat that kept my ears warm.

'You're blonde,' he said, in an 'I should have known' voice, as my hair fell down around my neck.

'I know that,' I assured him, rapidly losing the smile and setting to work rubbing the dogs down with a pile of old towels left for the purpose. I knew my limitations. Blonde jokes I could do without. 'Is that a problem?'

He didn't answer, or move for what seemed like for ever, then he said, 'Second floor, first door on the right.'

'Gabriel?' He paused in the doorway, half turned. 'Can I make you some toast or something?'

'Will you take any notice if I say no?'

'Probably not.'

'Then, providing you don't mind wasting your time, I won't waste my breath.' Wisely, he chose not to hang around for an argument.

So much for intimacy. And he hadn't smiled back.

'That's us women,' I said to Percy as I carefully cleaned his paws. 'Tiresome creatures who always think we know what's best for a man.' Unlike men, who never did. 'Although, come to think of it, that sounded suspiciously like a roundabout way of saying yes, don't you think?' Being a man, he couldn't just come out and say it.

Percy, bless him, licked my neck, which I knew meant he agreed with me. I gave him and Joe a hug and promised I'd be back later. Then I went through into the kind of kitchen that I'd only ever seen featured in lifestyle magazines. The kind that looked as if it had never seen a frying pan in action.

The fridge, however, was well stocked with the kind of expensive organic stuff that a food-conscious hostess would offer her guests. Maybe I was letting my prejudices get out of hand. Gabriel York's sister-in-law was probably a very nice woman when she wasn't burdened with unwanted guests. Especially when two of them were very lively dogs.

I knew from experience exactly what kind of mess two dogs could make.

I filled the kettle with filtered water, sliced stone-ground organic bread and placed it in the toaster. I found a tray and set out a glass of freshly squeezed orange juice—could it be freshly squeezed from a plastic bottle?—and added French butter and English marmalade. I did consider boiling one of the fat brown organic free-range eggs nestling in what looked like genuine straw, but decided that was just asking for abuse. Tomorrow, I promised myself as I poured the tea. I'd advance to an egg tomorrow.

I carried the tray up three flights of stairs and congratulated myself on the fact that I could save money on gym membership. I wasn't going to need to belong to a gym if I kept this up.

Gabriel York had, fortunately, left the door open, so I didn't have to use my foot to knock. Nevertheless, I thought it wise to advertise my presence before I went barging in.

'Gabriel?'

No reply. I put my head around the door and saw why. He'd flopped on top of the bed and fallen asleep. I put the tray down on a table by the window, then quietly cleared the night table so I could leave it close to hand for him when he woke. At least the orange juice would still be okay…

'What are you doing?'

I jumped, and a book slid on the floor. 'Trying not to wake you,' I offered as I bent to pick it up. Scarcely a little light sick room reading. It was a text book. Tropical medicine. Good grief, what on earth had he got?

'Then you failed.'

I put the book back and said, 'You know, it's a good job you're sick, or people might just tell you that you've got a serious problem with your inter-personal skills.'

He glowered at me. 'Is that right?'

'They might even say you're a bad-tempered grouch.'

'But only if I wasn't sick?'

'Very sick,' I amended, thoroughly fed up with his irritability. He might be having a hard time, but he didn't have to take it out on me. 'Fatal would just about cover it,' I added, under my breath.

'Not this time,' he replied. Clearly his hearing wasn't impaired. 'Although malaria is tricky. It will kill a fit man in days if it goes to the brain.'

'Malaria?' Good grief, I hadn't meant it. He looked bad, but not that bad… 'I thought you could take something to prevent that.'

'You can. It isn't infallible. Especially if you don't take it. This is a serious case of physician heal thy-self…' He finally managed something approaching a smile. It was worth the effort. The lines carved into his cheeks turned from haggard to rugged and it lit up his incredibly dark eyes in a way that more than made up for the sallow complexion.

I finished clearing a space for the tray and placed it beside him. 'You're a doctor?' I asked. 'I'm sure the agency said mister.'

'They would. I'm a surgeon.'

'Oh.' Which explained the bedtime reading. 'Why?'

'Why am I a surgeon?'

'No. Why is it mister? For surgeons? They don't do that in the US, do they?'

'You've lived there?'

'No, but I've watched *ER* on the television and...' I stopped, realising just how stupid that must sound.

'You know how the British like to be different,' he said, pushing himself up against the headboard. 'You may have noticed, while you were watching television, that we drive on the wrong side of the road, too.' My foolishness had at least raised another of those rare smiles. Even if it was at my expense, it was worth it. 'Are you going to give me that cup of tea, or is it just for decoration?'

'Oh, sorry.' I handed him the cup and saucer. He took the cup and I spooned sugar in until he told me to stop. My instincts were all urging me to say that so much sugar was not good for him. Luckily my will-power roused itself sufficiently to suggest that, since he was a doctor, he almost certainly knew that, and I kept quiet.

'Toast?' I didn't wait for a reply, but applied butter and marmalade, cut the slice of toast neatly in two, handed him one half and bit into the other half myself. I thought he'd be more likely to eat if he had company. Actually, all that organic stuff tasted pretty good. I just wished I'd brought up my tea, too. 'It's a long time since breakfast,' I said in response to a slightly ironic look. I didn't add that I hadn't actually eaten any breakfast. I didn't want any of that 'most important meal of the day' stuff. I was the one doing disapproving here.

'Help yourself. But sit down and take your time or you'll get indigestion.' He moved his long legs over to make room for me. Maybe I hesitated, feeling just the teeniest bit self-conscious about sitting on the bed of a man I scarcely knew—at least while he was in occupation—because somewhat irritably he added, 'That's my professional opinion. I won't charge you. This time.'

I sat.

CHAPTER FOUR

'WHERE did you get malaria?' I asked, in an attempt to distract myself. Which was ridiculous. I was twenty-five, for heaven's sake. And a day. It wasn't as if he was naked. Apart from his feet. He had excellent feet. Big without being excessive. And long sexy toes. They matched the long sexy fingers which were curled tightly around the cup.

He was, however, in no state to jump me. And he couldn't have made it any plainer that he didn't want to. Which was good.

I didn't want to be responsible for setting back his recovery.

'I mean, it isn't like the common cold,' I said, reverting to the distraction of malaria. 'You aren't likely to pick it up in Belgravia, are you?'

'I don't live in Belgravia.' He shrugged when I refused to be distracted into asking him where he did live. I'd get to that later. 'I was in West Africa, working with a medical charity. I spend a couple of weeks every year with them, doing cataract ops.' He was an eye surgeon, then... 'Did.'

'You don't think they'll let you do it again? Not even if you promise to be good and take your medicine?'

He finished the piece of toast he'd been holding for ever. I got the distinct feeling that he found it easier to eat than answer my question.

'So,' I said, buttering a second piece of toast and delaying the moment when, inevitably, I would put my head on the block. I cut it in two, but didn't hand him his share. I knew better than to try to force-feed invalids. I was hoping he'd take it just to be awkward. Being a man. 'Why didn't you take the stuff that would have protected you from getting it? Malaria?'

'The side effects were making it difficult to work, and the truth of the matter is that you just never think it will happen to you.'

I opened my mouth to say that he, if anyone, should have known better. And that there had to have been an alternative. Which he would have known a lot more about than me.

'Men are so useless. You need a wife to take care of you,' I said. Then, well aware that I was overstepping my dog-walker role, bit down on the toast. He wouldn't throw me out while I was eating. I'd definitely get indigestion...

He gave me an old-fashioned look. Well, it was a pretty old-fashioned idea.

'That's a somewhat un-PC notion. Are you volunteering?' he asked.

'Well, that would solve a lot of my problems,' I replied. I could get control of my trust fund and give up dog-walking as a career. On the other hand... 'But it would also present me with a whole new set.'

'All of them man-sized?'

'Quite. It's yet another example of the inequality of the sexes. Women don't actually need husbands, you see. We know how to take care of ourselves. Although I must admit I've heard a few career women remark that they could do with a wife of their own to handle all the tedious details of life. But men need wives. Take you, for instance.'

'I promise you, I'm managing well enough without one.'

'Oh, I don't mean just for sex,' I said, irritated that he was reducing my beautiful theory to the basics, then found myself blushing.

'Oddly enough, neither did I,' he replied, having to put a real effort into not showing his amusement. Which was not the same as smiling.

'I only meant,' I said, 'that if you'd had a wife she'd have made sure you took your anti-malaria drugs.' He was about to object, but I hadn't finished. 'And if they'd had side effects that bothered you she'd have made it her business to find something else that didn't.' Then, well into my stride, I added, 'And if she couldn't find anything suitable she'd have made sure she lost your passport.'

He concentrated on his tea. 'There's a flaw in your argument. That kind of wife has gone out of fashion.'

'How do you know? Have you been looking?'

'No. The last thing on earth I need is a wife. A marriage needs to be worked at. Requires serious emotional input.'

'So? It's not exactly hard labour.'

'No,' he said. 'But one in three marriages end in divorce.' Heavy on the irony, there. 'Of course my family is doing its best to buck the national average.'

He was divorced?

'Oh…sugar.' Me and my big mouth. He was sick, and instead of cheering him up I was adding to his depression. 'I'm sorry. I didn't mean… I should go.' I made a move, but he caught my arm, stopped me.

'Don't apologise, Sophie. It's scarcely your fault. It's just something of a family failing.' His hand lingered longer than was strictly necessary, and as if he couldn't think what else to do with it he finally reached out and took the other triangle of toast. 'Stay and finish your breakfast,' he said.

'What about your brother?' I said, gesturing at the house around us. I took the view that since he'd asked me to stay I had been given tacit permission to continue with the conversation. 'He's married.'

He looked at me with something close to exasperation. 'Tell me why we're having this conversation.'

'Unlike you,' I informed him, 'I have excellent inter-personal skills—a fact you might mention to that woman from the agency if she asks if I did a good job. People talk to me. You were telling me about your brother?' I prompted, before doing as I was told and taking another bite of toast.

He surrendered without a fight. Well, he was sick, poor man. 'Michael and Crissie live detached lives. They share a house, a bed, but precious little else. As a family we tend to be single-minded in our pursuit of a goal. And it's not just the men. The women are as bad. The people who make the mistake of loving us tend to get brushed aside by the slip-stream. Crissie only survives because she's like us. Totally single-minded in pursuit of her objective.'

On the point of allowing myself to be side-tracked with a Which is…?, I stopped myself. I wasn't interested in his sister-in-law. I wanted to know about him. 'You have sisters?'

'One. She's a politician.'

'Really? Would I have heard of her?' His expression suggested I think for a moment, and when my brain ran its memory program it didn't have to work too hard to come up with Jessica York. The woman everyone was watching as she rose to the top faster than Jersey cream. 'Jessica York is your sister?'

'My *divorced* sister.'

'I didn't know she was ever married.'

'She wasn't for long. Her husband caught her very young. She rapidly outgrew him.'

'Oh.'

'My mother is a lawyer,' he said, without waiting for me to ask. 'She led a campaign for equal rights for women in the workplace. Now she's a member of a government think-tank on women's issues. And, incidentally, also divorced.'

'I'm almost afraid to ask what your father does.'

'Irons his own shirts?' he offered. Then shook his head. 'No, of course he doesn't. He has a housekeeper to take care of the boring details and a series of charming lady-friends to take care of his other needs. He's a heart surgeon.'

'You take after him?'

'I've chosen to leave out the broken marriage.'

He *wasn't* divorced...

'Can you do that?' I asked. 'What happens when you fall in love?'

'I don't. It isn't compulsory.'

'I didn't realise there was a choice.' Then, in case he decided this was an invitation to switch the conversation to my own romantic attachments, or lack of them, I said, 'You're making a big mistake, you know. Married men live longer than bachelors simply because they have someone who cares enough to sweat the small stuff for them.'

'Is that right?'

'There are statistics,' I assured him.

My father had never had to give one thought to the details in his entire married life. How long would he manage before he started going downhill without my mother to take care of him? Or me.

Not wanting to go on that particular guilt trip, I offered Gabriel the last piece of toast, but as he reached to take it he lost control of the cup in his other hand and it tilted, spilling warm tea into his lap.

He let rip with one short but telling word, then flung himself off the bed and began to rip off the soaked bottoms.

I had one glimpse of long, hairy legs before I busied myself retrieving the cup, pulling off the cover before the tea soaked through to the sheets. I dashed downstairs with it, and by the time I'd stuffed it in the washing machine, found the soap and worked out the right program, he'd followed me down and added his tracksuit bottoms to the machine.

'I don't think that should go in with something white,' I protested.

His only response was to hit the 'on' switch.

'I'll, um, go and get the tray, shall I?'

'Leave it.'

'Right. Well, I'd better go,' I said, not really wanting to leave Gabriel alone. Hoping that he'd ask me to stick around. 'Will you be all right on your own?'

'I have a feeling that I'll be a lot safer that way. You are not good for my health.' I thought that was unfair, but didn't argue. Clearly my expression had other ideas. 'You're here to walk the dogs, Sophie, not fuss around me.'

Someone should. 'I thought the point of you staying here was to have someone on hand.'

'Then you thought wrong. It was to get me out of hospital. I don't need anyone mopping my fevered brow.'

I'd been that obvious?

'Go and do whatever you do with the rest of your day. Crissie's daily will be here any minute, and my brother will look in at lunchtime to ensure that the dogs don't wreck the designer garden while they have a comfort break.'

'Well, that's something, I suppose.' There was a pen and a notepad beside the kitchen phone. I wrote down my phone number, tore off the sheet and gave it to him. He took it, and I saw that he was shivering. 'You should put something on your feet.' He stuffed the paper into his pocket. 'If he can't make it, call me, okay? Don't go falling downstairs or passing out again.' I didn't wait for him to tell me he was perfectly able to manage, but headed for the door. 'I'll be back this evening.' I looked back, still reluctant to go. 'Is there anything I can bring you?'

I got a raised eyebrow for my trouble. 'Such as?'

'I don't know. A little light reading, perhaps? Medical text books are notoriously bad for your health. What about the latest Clancy or Grisham?' He didn't look impressed. Tired of putting myself out constantly for someone who couldn't be bothered to say thank you, even if it was coupled with no, I said, 'Maybe you'd prefer something off the top shelf? I won't tell your sister-in-law…'

He opened his mouth as if to say something. Then, no doubt deciding that discretion was probably the better part of whatever, paused before saying, 'No. Thank you.'

Even grouches could be brought to good manners with a little shove in the right direction.

'What about a video? Something to make you laugh.'

'Crissie doesn't have a television.'

'Oh.' His brother and sister-in-law might be very nice people—I was reserving judgement on that one—but they wouldn't be my choice of convalescent heaven.

Obviously he didn't have a choice.

'I've got a little portable set I could spare,' I offered.

'No, thank you. I'll survive.'

'A radio? A CD-player?' I was on a roll, going for the thank-you hat-trick. 'That's my final offer...'

'Just bring yourself,' he growled. 'And try to get here on time.'

'You can count on me.'

'I won't hold my breath.'

The internet agency was as good as its word. It had flooded my inbox with job opportunities, each one more unspeakably depressing than the one before. It was possible that by the time I'd worked to the end of them the first job would, in contrast, suddenly become so appealing that I'd beg for an interview. Maybe that was the plan.

I called the 'work at home' ad, hoping for something more exciting, but it turned out to be a scheme where I sent them money for a start-up kit of stuff to put together. Whilst I might not be a genius, it did occur to me that this was not the way it was supposed to work. I thanked them politely, but declined this fabulous opportunity to make them richer at my expense. And afterwards I reported them to the Trading Standards Office. There had to be a law…

I was trying to decide whether I'd rather be 'bright and articulate' in telesales—which was apparently the only growth industry at the moment—or if I wanted to embrace a career selling mobile phones, when my own phone rang.

'Sophie Harrington?' Miss Frosty. I felt the chill emanating from the earpiece of my phone. 'Lucy Cartwright.'

'Miss Cartwright.' All other contacts I'd had with agencies had been on a matey first-name basis. I just couldn't imagine ever calling this woman Lucy. 'Good morning.' One has to observe the civilities even when 'good' is a blatant exaggeration.

'I've got another little part-time job which might suit you. Bloomers need someone immediately, and remembering your enthusiasm for flower-arranging I naturally thought of you.'

'Oh!' Golly. *Bloomers!* They were the most seriously upmarket florists in London. My birthday sunflowers and roses had come from there. It seemed that I'd totally misjudged the woman. 'How kind of you.'

'Not at all. You'll have to work after the shop has closed, of course. Will that be a problem?'

'Er, no…'

'It's only temporary,' she warned. 'While their cleaner is off for some minor op. You start at six this evening. Someone will be there to show you what's required.' Maybe my underwhelmed silence warned her that suddenly I wasn't as totally thrilled, because she said, 'Of course, if you're too busy just say...'

This woman had a way of leaving me speechless that I was beginning to find extremely annoying. Since I was fairly sure that was her intention, I confined my response to a polite, 'Not at all.'

I took down the details, writing them beneath the dog-walking job. They were, at least, within easy walking distance of each other.

Dog-walker and cleaner. As a career plan it didn't exactly sparkle with prospects. But it could be worse. I was building a portfolio of jobs. I might not earn much, but I was going to be very fit.

The doorbell rang. Since no one had buzzed up from the entrance I assumed it was my 'guests' returning early from their country break only to discover that they'd forgotten their key.

It wasn't them. It was Aunt Cora, my mother's flighty younger sister; although, considering my mother's recent behaviour, maybe they were more alike than I'd imagined. It had just taken Mum longer to get going.

'Cora, what a lovely surprise!' I gave her a huge hug. Everyone needs an aunt like Cora. Generous, outrageous, full of fun. I adored her. 'Why didn't you call? How long are you staying?'

'It's a flying visit, darling. I've booked us a table for lunch at Giovanni's.' She regarded my sloppy attire with the critical eye of a woman who'd never been seen outside her own bathroom without a full make-up job. 'Did you know you've got a dirty mark on your chin?'

I rubbed at it, then wished I hadn't. 'Actually, it's a bruise.' She gave me a look that suggested no woman in control of her life would ever get a bruise on her chin. 'It's a long story—'

'Then save it for over lunch. I've got a taxi waiting.'

I didn't have time to do anything fancy with my hair, so I just brushed it and, since the curls were beginning to corkscrew wildly, fastened it back in a big ebony clasp. I dabbed concealer on my chin, to cover the bruise, and confined my make-up to a quick pass with mascara and lipstick, then slipped into a simple grey trouser suit and a pair of slender heels. Ten minutes later we were on our way.

'So? Flying visit?' I prompted.

She pressed a small jeweller's box into my hand. 'Happy birthday for yesterday.'

Did I say she was generous? The box contained an exquisite Victorian pendant set with amethysts and pearls. 'This is so lovely, Cora.'

'It belonged to your great-grandmother. She gave it to me when I got married.' She shrugged. 'The first time.'

And I found myself thinking of Gabriel. Committed never to marrying rather than risk failure, pain, heartache. Even if it was someone else's. I'd suggested that he was wrong, but I was no better...

'I was planning on giving it to you on your wedding day, but hardly anyone seems to bother with the formalities these days. Such a shame. There are pitifully few good excuses left for being totally extravagant with a hat.'

'I'm sorry to be such a disappointment,' I said, having to hunt for a smile. 'But thank you for a gorgeous present.'

'Oh, I haven't given up on you entirely. One of these days you'll meet someone else.'

'Someone else?'

'And stop pining over that Fotheringay boy.'

. Which dealt with my smile. How could she possibly know? 'I'm not—' But she stopped me, patting my hand.

'Don't worry. I'm the only one who connected the fact that you left home when his engagement was announced. Or notices that you have a lot of boyfriends but no one who gets close enough to touch.' And, as if she hadn't just dropped a small bombshell, she went on, 'So, in the meantime, rather than let this moulder in a box I decided to give it to you now.'

'Well, thank you. I'll treasure it.'

'Just so long as you don't treat it like the crown jewels and keep it for state occasions. Make the most of it while your neck is still in good shape.'

All of a sudden I had the feeling that this wasn't going to be such a fun treat after all, but I told her about Kate's pot of anti-wrinkle cream and that made her laugh. Then we arrived at Giovanni's and conversation was put on hold while we decided what to eat.

'So,' I said, when we'd ordered and Cora seemed unusually quiet. 'What's the occasion? Adorable though you are, I can't believe you flew from the South of France for the day simply to give me a birthday present that you could just as easily have sent by courier.'

'No.' She sighed. 'Look, there's no easy way to say this, Sophie. My investments haven't been doing so well lately. I'm going to have to use the flat to top up my income.'

My mouth dried. What was it I'd been saying about things not getting worse?

'You want to let it?' I asked. 'At the market rate?' Wondering how on earth I could raise that kind of money.

She didn't answer immediately. All around us the restaurant hummed with people having a good time, leaving our table a little bubble of silence.

Heart sinking, I continued, 'You've already let it?'

'Actually, darling, I've sold it. Nigel and Amber just fell in love with it, you see. They've been looking everywhere for something that would come close, but you know how it is when you've seen somewhere perfect. Nothing else will do.'

I understood the concept very well. Perry Fotheringay had been perfect. I'd tried looking for someone else who would come close, too. But it was more than just his good looks. It was chemistry. A kind of recognition...

Without warning Gabriel York's glowering face was filling my head. His irritable growl as he pushed away help. Nothing could be further from Perry's soft teasing laughter, sparkling come-and-get-me eyes, yet my pulse-rate lifted until it was thudding through my ears as if I was still breathing my own life into his body.

'They've been pushing me and pushing me for

weeks.' Cora's voice broke through, bringing me back to reality. 'I imagine they think I've just been waiting for a bigger offer, but honestly until last week I wasn't interested. A meeting with my accountant has put a different complexion on things.'

'Oh, Cora, I'm so sorry.'

She put on a brave smile. 'A little temporary difficulty, that's all. Anyway, I'm here to sign the contracts. The completion date is down to you.'

She wanted to know how quickly I could move out. Clearly, for her sake, the sooner the better. 'It'll take me a day or two to pack. The weekend?'

'So soon? That would be wonderful.'

I sat back, momentarily winded. By the weekend I was going to be homeless. I could scarcely believe it. My house guests—who'd conveniently gone away for a week so they wouldn't be around when Cora broke the news—had bought my home from under me.

'It's not as if you could afford to stay there by yourself, Sophie,' Cora pointed out gently. 'Not now your father has suspended your trust income.' And how did she know about that? 'You haven't even got a job at the moment.'

'No, but—' About to tell her about my plans to sub-let Kate's room, I stopped myself. Cora had generously let us use her flat for years, asking nothing more than that we covered all the running costs. Now she needed the money, and the least I could do was make this as painless as possible for her. 'But that's just a little temporary difficulty,' I replied, echoing her own sentiments and managing to find a smile from somewhere. 'I'm more concerned about you.'

'No, no. You mustn't worry. I'll just have to be a

little less extravagant for a while.' Then, 'Why don't you go home for a while, Sophie?' This was beginning to sound like a conspiracy. Except Cora would never do that to me. She sounded genuinely concerned as she said, 'Your father really needs you. He's falling apart without your mother.'

Of course he was. He'd never once in all his married life reached for a clean shirt and not found one ready and waiting. She'd run the house, the church social committee, the community council, the whole village, for heaven's sake, practically single-handed. She'd given and given and given, until one day she'd found herself on the receiving end of a little attention for a change. It had gone to her head. And would undoubtedly end in tears.

'He's not the only one who misses her,' I said. 'Maybe instead of sitting at home feeling sorry for himself Dad should break the habit of a lifetime and go after her—tell her how much she means to him. Show her how much he needs her.'

'That's a no, I take it?'

I stifled a sigh. It would be so easy. No worries about a job. No worries about where to live. Just while I got my act together. The career plan. The life plan.

Too easy. And not just for me.

'I can't replace my mother. And I won't be doing Dad any favours by offering him a crutch to lean on. He needs to face up to what's happened and move on. We all do.' Cora winced at my thoughtless choice of words and, feeling guilty, I said, 'Don't worry. It isn't a problem. I can bunk with a mate while I look for somewhere more within my means. You can tell

Nigel and Amber that it's safe to come back. One way or another, I'll be gone by Saturday.' I stood up, suddenly oppressed by the noise of the restaurant, needing to get some air. 'Look, I'm going to have to run.'

Cora hugged me. 'Thank you for being so sweet about this.'

'No, thank *you*. You've been brilliant and we've taken you horribly for granted. If I can do anything, any time, you only have to ask.'

'In that case, do you really have to rush off? I'm not leaving until this evening. We could go shopping,' she said, totally incorrigible. So much for being less extravagant.

'Haven't you got to see your lawyer? Sign contracts?' I reminded her, resisting temptation without too much difficulty. One of us had to be responsible. Since the older generation seemed to have lost the plot, it was down to me.

'Ten minutes, tops,' she promised.

'I'm really sorry, Cora. I'd love to keep you company, but I've got a date with a couple of hounds who'll chew the legs off the kitchen table unless I'm on time to take them for a run.' Keeping it light—not wanting her to feel that I was avoiding her company—I said, 'Of course, if you're really stuck for something to do, you're very welcome to join me.'

'Er, thanks, but I think I'll pass on that treat.'

'You don't know what you're missing.'

'Mud, mud, and more mud?' she offered. 'I'm not dressed for it.'

'Neither am I, which means I really have to dash or I'll be late again.'

And to think I'd been congratulating myself that things couldn't get worse. I really must learn to curb my optimism.

At least I wasn't late.

It was just as well. My arrival coincided with that of a taxi. I beat the driver to the bell and the door was immediately flung open by Gabriel York. He was wearing a long dark overcoat and looked as if he'd been pacing the hall, scarcely able to contain his impatience.

Pacing was clearly an exaggeration—he didn't look as if being on his feet was that bright an idea. But feverish energy radiated from him, and the small overnight bag at his feet suggested he had more than pacing in mind.

Percy and Joe were sitting—just—with their leads ready clipped to their collars, in keen anticipation of an outing. He handed me their leads without a word, then picked up the bag.

'Where on earth do you think you're going?' I demanded.

I hadn't had a good day so far, and I certainly wasn't taking any nonsense from a man who looked as if a puff of wind would blow him over.

'Home,' he said.

'Excuse me?'

'I'm going home,' he repeated slowly, as if I was dim.

This, I was sure, was not a great idea. Did his family know? 'Have you outworn your welcome?' I asked. 'What happened? Did Crissie find out about the bedcover? Did one of the dogs leave hair on the hall carpet? Eat the organic chicken?'

'Quite possibly all three.' He might have smiled, but he needed all his energy to keep on his feet. Anyone with a thimbleful of sense could see that he should be in bed, not moving house. 'But that's not the reason I'm going. My brother's flown to New York this afternoon. Some crisis at the UN that only he can handle, apparently. He didn't even have time to come home and fetch a toothbrush.'

'So?'

'Crissie's packing now so that she can follow him with his stuff.'

'Why? Don't they sell toothbrushes in New York?'

He stopped, finally looked at me. Since I was blocking his way, he didn't have a lot of choice about this. 'I'm sure they do, Sophie, but he's going to be away for at least a month and he'll need more than a toothbrush,' he explained, wearily patient. From somewhere inside the house I heard the rattle of coat hangers in freefall, followed by the exasperated scream of a woman at the end of her tether. 'As you can hear, she's got quite enough to cope with without having to worry about me.'

'Someone needs to,' I declared, absolutely twitching as every feminine instinct urged me to reach out, put my arm around him, take his weight on my shoulder and put him straight back to bed, where it was warm. Every feminine instinct also warned me that it was the worst thing I could possibly do.

'I can look after myself.'

'Oh, right.' I injected a certain amount of disbelief into my voice.

As if to prove my scepticism, he took a step towards the door and swayed noticeably. Oh, to hell with it. He wasn't in any shape to argue. I stepped up to him and tucked myself beneath his arm, keeping tight hold of the dogs with the other hand.

'You need to sit down,' I said.

'In the taxi,' he said, with grim determination, and while he didn't exactly push me away there was only one direction he was going to allow me to take him in.

'You should have phoned me,' I said, when he was sitting inside the cab. 'I could have been here earlier.'

'I tried. Your phone was switched off.' He made it sound as if I'd done this deliberately, just to thwart him.

'It most certainly was not,' I declared, and fished it out of my pocket just to prove it. I was right. It wasn't switched off. But the battery was dead. 'Oh, knickers.'

'I left a message on your voice-mail,' he said, manfully resisting the temptation to say what was clearly at the forefront of his mind.

'It's rapidly turning into that sort of week,' I said. 'There are probably dozens of people trying to phone me and offer me jobs right now...'

'Really?'

'No. Just wishful thinking.' I put the phone away and looked at him. 'Are you sure you should be doing this? You look terrible.'

'I feel terrible. Talking to you isn't helping.' He held out a piece of paper with an address and phone number written on it. 'Take the dogs for their run and then bring them home. This is the address.'

'Only if you promise me you'll go straight to bed when you get there. Leave the door on the latch and I'll let myself in.'

He looked as if he was about to argue, but contented himself with muttering, 'Bossy cow.'

'Technically, that would be heifer,' I replied, closing the door before giving the driver the address.

CHAPTER FIVE

I WAITED until the taxi was out of sight, then went back up the steps to shut the front door. But before I could do that Cristabel York appeared at the foot of the stairs.

'Has he gone?' She looked surprised. 'Damn the man. He didn't even bother to say goodbye.'

'I think he decided you had other things on your mind.'

'You don't have to make excuses for him. He wouldn't bother to do it for himself, believe me.' She brushed her sleek hair back from her face, leaving it ruffled and untidy, and quite suddenly she looked human. Vulnerable. Exhausted. 'This is a nightmare. York men individually are difficult to live with, but two of them under one roof are more than flesh and blood can stand.'

Technically, right now she didn't have any. But I kept that thought to myself. I thought I'd probably gone about as far I could safely travel on the technical front.

'They must have some good points,' I offered. I felt honour-bound to defend Gabriel; he was my employer, after all. Although since she was married to his brother she presumably knew what she was talking about.

'Oh, they're absolute bristling with good points,' she agreed. 'They're forceful, dynamic, totally irresistible forces of nature who, once they've set their minds on a goal, are unstoppable in its pursuit. That's why I'm married to one of them. That's what makes them totally impossible to live with. I have a career. I have a business to run. But does that count for anything? No, I have to drop everything to fit in with Michael's personal mission to save the world. At least Gabe has had the decency not to inflict himself on a wife…' Perhaps she realised that she was running on in front of a complete stranger and she let it go. 'Sorry. You don't want to hear this. But, really, I'm not the uncaring bitch my brother-in-law would have you believe. He not only doesn't want anyone to care, he positively discourages any hint of concern.'

I'd noticed, but I just said, 'I can quite see that with a couple of dogs in tow he doesn't make the ideal house guest.'

'If he'd just stayed put in hospital until he was fit enough to be left on his own…' She threw up her hands. 'Not him. He couldn't be that reasonable. But then doctors notoriously make the worst patients. As for the dogs…I thought bringing them here would help him settle, feel at home.'

She'd brought them?

'Where were they? While he was away?'

'Staying with a colleague. A nurse. The ideal solution would have been for him to move in with her, but of course that would have been too simple. He wouldn't hear of it.'

He'd lied about the kennels…

She shook her head. 'I'm being too hard on him. He was so depressed he couldn't think straight. It's one of the after effects of malaria, apparently. Did he tell you he'd had malaria?'

I nodded.

'Well, as I said, I thought it would help.'

'I'm sure it has.'

'Do you think so?' That seemed to cheer her momentarily. Then, 'Now he insists on going home. Wretched, stubborn man. He could have stayed here. My cleaner would have come in every day to check up on him. Make sure he had something to eat. He really shouldn't be on his own.'

'No.' We were in total agreement on that one.

'Well, at least he'll have you popping in twice a day to make sure he hasn't passed out again.' She grabbed a pen from the table by the telephone and jotted something on a notepad. 'Look, this is our number in New York,' she said, tearing off a sheet of paper and offering it to me. 'If there's a problem, ring me—okay?'

I had the feeling I was getting deeper into this than I wanted to go. Risking more than life and limb... *Limbs* mended.

'Look, I'm just the dog-walker,' I said, as self-preservation asserted itself. I was about to suggest that Mrs York's cleaner could still pop in to see him every day—he was only down the road in Pimlico—when the dogs, alerted by this reference to walks, began to make encouraging little yelps and tug impatiently on their leads.

'That's why you're the perfect person to keep an eye on him,' Crissie York said, seizing the initiative. 'Those wretched dogs are the only things he cares about and he can't take them out himself.' Gabriel was right—it wasn't only the York men who were unstoppable in the pursuit of what they wanted. 'If he's rude, just remember that and tell him to get lost.'

'If?' I enquired, finding myself warming to the woman, despite her attempt to entangle me in her personal crisis.

'Don't worry, I'll sort it out with the agency. Pay for any extra time.'

'No. Don't do that.' I was reluctant to get that closely involved. I had, as Cora had suggested, built a protective wall about myself. The minute I'd started worrying about Gabriel York I'd felt the foundations being undermined. 'Isn't there anyone else?'

She ignored my obvious desperation, just continued to hold out the piece of paper. Unstoppable in her persistence. And if there had been anyone else she wouldn't have asked a total stranger, would she?

It wasn't so much the responsibility that bothered me, but I was supposed to be job-hunting. Flat-hunting. Moving.

'Please?'

I was a sucker for a please. And what else could I do? I had to go there twice a day to take the dogs out, anyway. How much more work would it be to check up on him? Make sure he had something for breakfast. Get him a ready-meal from the supermarket to stick in the microwave for supper, perhaps.

I took the piece of paper, tucked it into my kitty notebook and pushed it into my pocket.

'I'll do what I can.'

'Great.' She opened her purse and thrust some money into my hand. 'This will cover any expenses. If it comes to more I'll pay you when I get back.'

'No...' This wasn't a job like dog-walking or cleaning. It would be completely wrong to take money for doing what a good neighbour would do. But the phone began to ring and she reached for it, waving her thanks as she kicked the door shut.

Percy and Joe had a somewhat curtailed gallop in the grounds of the Royal Hospital, Chelsea—which confusingly wasn't a hospital at all, but a retirement home for old soldiers. I had to find Gabriel's place in Pimlico—he'd only given me the address, no directions—and I didn't want to leave it too long. Heaven alone knew what state he'd be in when I got there.

Then I had to get to Bloomers for six o'clock and put in a couple of hours of cleaning before going home to start packing.

Gabriel lived in a mews cottage—whitewashed on the outside and the door painted black, but long enough ago to have lost the gloss, with brass fittings that hadn't seen metal polish in living memory. He didn't go in for tortured greenery on the doorstep, either. There was a stone pot, but whatever had been planted in it had long since died. He had remembered to leave the door on the latch, however, and the dogs, thrilled to be home, raced through the rooms, turning dizzy circles with excitement.

'Gabriel?' I had at the most twenty minutes in which to give the dogs some water and make sure he hadn't collapsed before I had to leave in time to make it to Bloomers.

I turned on the cold tap to let the water run for a minute while I looked around. Amazingly the place had a little garden at the rear, and the dogs had an

electronic flap triggered by a device on their collars
to let themselves in and out. Hardly the same as living
in the country, but a lot better than being shut up in
someone else's utility room.

I filled the bowls, set them down and, since I'd had
no response from the boss, went to look for him.

It was a totally masculine cottage, with the whole
of the ground floor given over to the kind of kitchen
that was a genuine comfort zone, with a couple of
armchairs and an ancient sofa covered by a throw.
The dogs flung themselves onto it.

I found Gabriel in the rear bedroom.

He must have been feeling bad, because for once
in his life he'd done exactly what he'd been told and
put himself to bed. Well, no. That was a bit of an
exaggeration. What he'd actually done was kick off
his shoes, wrap himself in a duvet and fallen asleep
still wearing his coat.

I didn't think it was a good idea to leave him that
way but, checking my watch, realised I didn't have
time to do anything about it right then. I'd have to
come back.

I shrugged. I was always going to have to come
back. Make sure he was okay. In the meantime I had
to get to Bloomers. If I ran all the way I might just
make it.

I paused just long enough to scribble a note in my
kitty notebook, tear it out and leave it propped up by
the bedside lamp.

I'll be back.

As I let myself out, leaving the door on the latch
and relying on the dogs to deter unwelcome visitors,

it occurred to me that it had sounded more like a threat than a promise.

The ladies at Bloomers were totally brilliant.

I didn't realise they'd still be working so late—to be honest I didn't know what to expect, having never done anything like this before—but there were three of them, bundled up in coats against the chill, hands red from close contact with cold water as they plucked flowers from the surrounding buckets.

They took one look at me, flushed of face, bent practically double as, clutching my midriff, I gasped out my apology for being three minutes late, and immediately took me under their collective wing.

'You sit there and get your breath back. I dare say we could all do with a tea break. Greta, put that kettle on.'

'I'm sorry, really. I don't want to keep you waiting…'

'It's not a problem. We're going to be here half the night preparing everything for this wedding, anyway. So long as the shop gets cleaned it doesn't matter whether it's at six o'clock or seven, does it?'

'It doesn't?'

Actually, now I'd recovered sufficiently to concentrate on something other than the simple act of breathing, I could see what they meant. The floor of the preparation room behind the shop was all but hidden by buckets of flowers, and one of the girls was putting together those beribboned posies for the pew-ends of a church at a speed that made me blink.

'Wow. Who's getting married? Royalty?'

'No, just some TFB. I don't know how much the

whole affair is costing, but I do know how much we're charging for the flowers and, believe me, I'm not complaining at having to work late.'

'TFB?'

'Trust Fund Babe,' the one called Greta replied with a grin as she placed a mug of tea in my hand. 'The kind of girl who's never going to have to turn out on a chilly late-November evening to mop floors for a living. Do you want sugar in that?'

I shook my head. A TFB.

That's what I was.

Without the TF.

I felt guilty sitting there, drinking the tea they'd made me, being made a fuss of as if I was one of them. A worker, rather than someone who'd taken her education, her advantages, totally for granted.

What on earth had I been doing with my life?

Flitting from job to job without a thought for the future, like some brainless butterfly.

Suddenly I saw myself through Miss Frosty's eyes and knew why she'd been so hard on me. She could have been a lot harder. This, as cleaning jobs went, wasn't that bad. In fact, having watched Greta and the rest of the girls, their hands red from cold, I decided that my job was pretty cushy in comparison and put my back into it.

They were still at it when I left, clutching a deliciously scented posy of trimmings. I'd been invited to help myself; it was one of the perks of the job, apparently. I could scarcely tell them that I already had two gorgeous arrangements they'd delivered to me the day before. They'd probably think I was some privileged idiot, slumming it for a bet or something, and despise me.

I'd put my hands up to the privileged idiot, but they were great women and I didn't want them to despise me, so I thanked them and took the flowers.

What I did need, though, was to find a bed before the weekend, and so far all I'd done was leave a message for Tony on his voice-mail. Even if he had called back, my cellphone battery was flatter than one of my mother's banqueting cloths. And I had to pack, too. But I couldn't even start to think about that until I'd checked on Gabriel.

I walked back to Pimlico, feeling a bit light-headed from the scent of so many lilies. Or maybe it was from lack of sleep. My feet didn't seem to be quite my own, and the pavement had a disconcerting tendency to come up to meet me. It was a relief to let myself back into the cottage, even though I didn't dare sit down. It was all I could do to push away the dogs, who'd rushed out of the kitchen to see whether they should eat me or love me. They decided to love me, presumably in the hope that I could be fooled into feeding them again.

I stuck the colourful posy in a jug, yawning widely as I headed for the stairs to see how Gabriel was doing. Definitely lack of sleep. I'd had a late night followed by an early morning and been on the go ever since.

His bedroom was cold—at some point he must have woken up, thrown open the window and taken off his coat—but he was restless and muttering incoherently. I laid my hand on his forehead and discovered that he was hot to the touch. Feverish.

I shut the window. While getting him cooled down was undoubtedly a priority, I was pretty sure he wouldn't appreciate a case of double pneumonia to add to his woes.

After that I set about prising the duvet from his grasp so that I could get him properly undressed. He was tangled up in it, and by the time I'd managed to get it free he wasn't the only one feeling the heat. Maybe the effort had exhausted him, too, though, because he was quieter after that, giving me a chance to unfasten the waistband of his trousers and ease them down his legs. Not that it was particularly easy. He was a dead weight. And they were long legs.

Eventually, though, I was done, and I left him stretched out on his back, wearing just his shirt and pair of clinging grey boxers that—well, clung. To a pair of undeniably sexy hips.

Not that I was in the slightest bit interested in his hips.

I dragged my gaze away from them and went back downstairs in search of something for him to drink. The fridge, inevitably, was empty, so he was going to have to make do with tap water.

Then, because there was no hot water in the tank, I had to heat some in a kettle to sponge him down with—just enough to take the chill off. My legs wobbling with fatigue, I finally climbed back up the stairs, feeling a bit like some poor relation out of a Victorian melodrama, delegated to sit by the invalid's bed and mop his forehead, waiting for the fever to break..

Too late. By the time I made it back to his bedside Gabriel had cooled down. More than cooled down. He was shivering uncontrollably.

Maybe at this point I should have given up and called an ambulance.

Maybe I should at least have *looked* for a hot water bottle, but frankly I didn't believe he would own such a thing. Besides, the thought of facing those stairs again was enough to make my legs buckle.

I don't know how many miles they'd walked—and run—that day, but believe me they'd done more than enough. If I went downstairs I wasn't sure I'd ever make it back up again.

Added to that, my back and arms ached from the unaccustomed wielding of an industrial-sized mop. As for my head…

Okay, you've got the picture.

It was warmth he needed. Right now. And I was warm.

And in desperate need of a lie-down.

Two birds with a single whatever.

I stripped off my trousers and sweater and fell into bed beside him, pulling the duvet up under his chin to warm him with my own body. I must have been paying more attention to those first aid lectures than I'd realised, because I remembered some stuff about heat transfer. Good for hypothermia. In an emergency.

Well, this was an emergency. And, lying sideways so that my cheek was pressed against his shoulder and my body was pressed firmly along the length of his, I pulled the quilt over us both and cradled him. It shouldn't take long. As soon as he stopped shivering I'd get up and go home.

*   *   *

'Tell me, did I miss something?'

I opened my eyes and found myself face to face with Gabriel York. He seemed bemused. Not bothered, you understand, but those dark eyes definitely betrayed a man who was in the throes of bemusement.

I could understand that. I struggled with bemusement myself for a moment or two while I mentally disentangled the events that had led to me to the point where I'd fallen into his bed, his arms.

By the time I remembered he'd got his expression under control, and that cool, slightly guarded look was firmly back in place. But I could have sworn that, just for a moment, he'd been smiling. Well, maybe not quite smiling, but there had been a slight softening of his mouth, something about the eyes that suggested he was definitely thinking about it.

And why not? He had every reason to smile.

It wasn't just my face that was—well, face to face with him. My entire body seemed to be pressed very firmly against his. Chest to chest. Thigh to thigh. Hip to, um, hip. And, well, *hellooo*. He was clearly feeling a lot better this morning. Because it was morning. And not particularly early, judging by the daylight pouring in through the windows. We'd slept through the entire night, wrapped close as lovers, as innocent as babes, in each other's arms.

Reality intruded. He was aroused, as any man might be if he woke and found a strange woman in his bed. That my own body, released from a long cold purdah, should respond with a similar heat, real physical desire, was considerably less expected. Breathstoppingly unexpected. Shockingly so. No, worse than shocking, because not only wasn't I making any move to distance myself from him, I didn't *want* to move. I wanted to be even closer...

'You, um, had a fever,' I said, in an attempt to distract myself. Well, I had to say something. 'You were shivering.'

'Is that right? And is this some new treatment that hasn't made it into the text books?'

There was a hint of something teasing in his voice, but like the smile it was buried deep. I was prepared to dig...

'It was an emergency,' I pointed out. 'This seemed like the most energy-efficient way of dealing with the situation.'

'Energy-efficient?'

That one had nearly got him. He was having to work at not smiling now. Encouraged, I said, 'It's called heat transfer.'

'I thought that was something to do with plumbing.'

Close...

'You're thinking of heat exchange.'

'I am?' He sounded surprised that I would know the difference. Well, heck, I was a blonde...

'I worked as a receptionist at a heating and ventilation company for a while.' A very short while. One of the directors had been very keen to explain all about heat exchange one night. After the office had closed.

'Oh, please, don't misunderstand me. I'm not complaining. This is much more, um, efficacious than being manhandled into an ambulance by a couple of burly paramedics and carted off to hospital.'

Efficacious?

Oh, no. I wasn't going to smile until he did. Close thing, though.

I cleared my throat, giving myself a moment to get my face under control. 'Actually, I did think about calling them.' Well, I had. Momentarily. Until I'd realised I'd have to go downstairs to use the phone. 'But since you'd undoubtedly refuse to go with them, for the second time in as many days, I decided I'd just get arrested for serially time-wasting the emergency services' overstretched resources. And I'm much too busy for that.'

'Doing what?'

He sounded genuinely interested. I suspected he was applying the same distraction technique…

'Finding a proper job—' as opposed to an improper one, where I ended up lying in bed with my boss '—preferably in the next twenty-four hours. Finding somewhere to live, ditto. Then there's walking your dogs twice a day. Oh, and cleaning a flower shop in the evening.'

'Busy schedule. And you've still found time to make it your personal responsibility to be my guardian angel.'

I didn't feel like an angel, but clearly it would not be in my best interests to tell him that. Probably. But with a name like Gabriel he would know more about it than me. 'Someone needs to be,' I said.

'Well, I'm glad it was you. You seem to have a natural gift for one-to-one caring.'

'Oh, it's not a gift. I did a first aid course. That's where I learned how to do CPR—'

'Believe me, you did *not* learn how to do CPR.'

'—and all about heat transfer.'

His smile hovered again. His face didn't change. There were none of those sexy crinkles that men do so beautifully—the kind that on women would just be crow's feet—but somewhere behind his eyes there was a warmth that betrayed him.

'Are you sure you learned this at first aid?' he enquired, with the barest suggestion of innuendo.

I swallowed. 'Absolutely. There was a section on improvisation. You know. If you're lost up a mountain, or something...'

'You cuddle together to keep warm. You seem to have grasped the principle with extraordinary enthusiasm.'

'No,' I said firmly. 'If someone falls, succumbs to hypothermia...' It occurred to me that, while I was probably talking utter nonsense, he was a professional and knew exactly what I was getting at.

It also occurred to me that the treatment had worked extremely well. He was looking and sounding a whole lot better this morning.

And maybe I should make a move.

'So, let's recap,' he said, clearly not done with teasing me.

No! Please don't let's recap!

'First there was your interesting version of mouth-to-mouth resuscitation. More commonly called the kiss of life...'

I let out a gasp that might have been of outrage as he bent without warning and brushed his dry lips over mine. The unexpected touch sent shock waves of warmth spreading through me and my body responded like the motor of a very expensive car, purring so quietly that you could hardly hear it, but ready to leap into action the moment pressure was applied to the accelerator...

'Did that work?'

Work? My heart, dormant and neglected, was pounding away like a jackhammer.

'You're a doctor. You have an unfair advantage.'

'Oh, I think we're about evens on that one. But the heat transfer is more difficult...' His arm, which was beneath me, with his hand spread over my back, tightened slightly. His other hand, which I belatedly realised was cupping my bottom, did the same.

It had not seemed possible that we could be any closer. But the difference was breathtaking.

Well, I was finding it hard to breathe anyway.

'I think perhaps we're both already warmer than is absolutely wise,' I managed.

Since I was the one who'd tucked up against him I realised I was in no position to complain. But enough was enough. Even if he was just teasing...

Teasing? The dour and grouchy doctor?

How likely was that?

Since the only alternative was that he was putting a move on me, I decided to bank on it. And stay put. Clearly any abrupt move to put some distance between us it would make altogether too much of it. But it was time to call a halt.

'In fact that's more than enough,' I said. Which was not true. I was fairly sure that I could take this kind of close encounter all day.

'Enough?'

'Dosage is critical,' I explained, with what I can only describe as admirable cool under the circumstances. The knee to breast contact. His warm breath tickling against my ear. The pulsing beat of his heart in counterpoint to mine… Even so, I was forced to swallow again before I said, 'Overdoing it will almost certainly lead to a relapse. Possibly even a return of the fever.'

I was not prepared to gamble on which of us would overheat, reach boiling point first.

'I suspect you're right.' He didn't move a muscle. Well, maybe just one… 'But it's almost worth having a relapse to see just how far you'd take this interesting therapy.'

'This is the end of the treatment session, Doctor.'

For a moment he held me hard up against him, his dark eyes unreadable, his face expressionless, any hint of warmth, a smile, long gone. My top had ridden up in the night, as had his shirt, and my bare stomach was pressed against his midriff, my thighs languorously soft against the hairy masculinity of his legs. Warm skin against warm skin. It felt dangerously thrilling, like balancing on the edge of a precipice. I just knew that one wrong move would lead to disaster.

Never had disaster seemed such an attractive proposition. All I had to do was lift my mouth to his, run my tongue along his sensuous lower lip and…

And he let me go.

I was lying in his bed, locked in his arms, letting my imagination run away with me, and he just…let me go.

He didn't move. He simply took his hands away in one clean movement, without allowing the one to trail enticingly down my leg or the other to ruffle against my hair.

My leg deeply regretted the omission.

My hair was already so ruffled that a little more wouldn't have made the slightest bit of difference.

My head, having taken due note of all of the above, appeared to have gone with the 'disaster' scenario. Or maybe it was too busy drowning in the forgotten sensory pleasure of a man's hard body against mine to send the 'move' signals to the rest of my body.

'It's nearly eight o'clock, Sophie. You do realise that you're going to be late for work again?'

Oh, well, that did it. Like a basinful of ice-cold water, it brought my head, my thighs, all those other wayward bits of me that hadn't been behaving for the last five minutes, right back into line, and I was out of his bed—and dearly wishing I was the kind of girl who kept a pair of clean knickers and a spare tooth-brush in her bag—before you could say Jack Robinson.

'You'll find my wallet in my coat,' he said. 'Take some money for a taxi home. The dogs can wait an hour.'

'You read minds?' I demanded.

'It's hardly mind-reading. When I've been working all night the only thing on my mind is to get home, take a shower—'

'Working?' I was outraged. 'I stopped working the minute I brought your dogs home, Mr York. This was… This was…'

I couldn't for the life of me think *what* it was, but I was damn certain it wasn't anything to do with work.

'Therapy?' he prompted. 'You'd better take my

keys, too,' he said, since I was clearly lost for words. 'So that you can let yourself back in.'

I was hopping on one leg as I tried to get the other one into the tangled mess of my jeans as quickly as possible. Sitting on the bed would have made it easier, but I wasn't going back there. Not until I'd given myself a refresher course in common sense.

And taken a shower. A cold one seemed like a sensible move.

But what he'd said about taking keys finally filtered through to my brain 'You're not planning on going out?' I demanded.

That shouldn't have been a question, I realised, so I rephrased it.

'You're *not* going out. You *are* staying in bed.'

My mind, clearly out on a limb and sawing off the branch behind it, chimed in with, Oh, right. And how are you going to make him do that?

Fortunately it was on its own. Or maybe Gabriel had decided to let me off the hook—however unlikely that seemed. Anyway, completely ignoring my concern for his health, he said, 'I'll find you the spare key later.'

That made me mad. I kept saving this man's life, for heaven's sake. I had every right to demand he took better care of it.

'I don't need a key. You are not—'

'No, Sophie. I'm not going out. I'm going to do exactly what the ministering angel ordered and stay put for a while. But you said you needed somewhere to stay temporarily and I've got a spare room. So use it.' He rolled over onto his back and closed his eyes, as if that was an end to the matter. Not quite. He added, 'That way you won't have any excuse to be late for work this evening. Or tomorrow.'

Did I say I'd been lost for words?

Wrong. They were positively tumbling over themselves to get off my tongue. Once I'd made up my mind between telling him what he could do with his spare room. Or possibly throwing my arms around his neck and thanking him.

I compromised. 'Are you hungry?'

'No. My appetite is zero. A side effect of malaria.' Along with depression. I reminded myself to look it up on the internet and see what else I could look forward to. 'Although if you're feeling in a ministering mood you could bring me another glass of water before you go.'

Reaching for the glass at his bedside, I realised it was empty. 'Oh, good, you found it—' I began. Then stopped. The glass was empty and there was a bottle of pills beside it that hadn't been there last night. Which meant that at some time in the night he'd woken up, got up and found his pills, and then got right back into bed, put his arm around me and gone back to sleep.

Perhaps he'd thought he was hallucinating...

'You can trust me,' he said, doing the mind-reading thing again.

'I know. You're a doctor...' I snapped.

'And you needn't worry that I'm looking for a nurse on the cheap.'

'Oh, well, fine. You're not getting one.' I fetched him a fresh glass of water, put it by the bed. 'I won't be long.'

He'd burrowed beneath the covers. 'Just feed the

dogs before you go, will you?' he muttered from the depths of his quilt.

Oh, crumbs. He was feeling rotten and I was giving him a hard time. I hovered for a minute, wondering what to do for the best, until he opened his eyes and said, 'Are you still here?'

'No,' I snapped, 'I'm just a figment of your imagination.'

He looked, for just a moment, as if he might take issue with me on that. But he must have decided it was too much effort and closed them again.

I took his keys and a twenty-pound note. I couldn't afford to be stupid about it and I really didn't see why his sister-in-law should subsidise his care in the community. Then I went downstairs, fed Percy and Joe and, since time was short, used the taxi ride to put in some work on a realistic assessment of my immediate choices.

I could sleep on Tony's sofa until I found somewhere within my budget—sound of hollow laughter here—which would no doubt please Tony.

I could go home. Which would certainly please my father. As well as my sister, my aunt and probably my mother. Everyone, in fact, I cared about.

I could take up Gabriel York's offer and use his spare room. Which would please no one.

CHAPTER SIX

THE first option was going to be uncomfortable, and might rekindle any hopes Tony had of getting me into his bed. It wouldn't be kind.

The second was just going to be admitting defeat. I'd rather take my chances on Tony's sofa. Besides, I'd meant what I'd said to Cora. It would allow Dad to put off confronting some pretty painful choices. He needed to get on with it. As I'd been forced to do.

That left the third option which was, no doubt about it, utterly stupid.

I didn't know anything about Gabriel York beyond the fact that he was an eye surgeon, had a brother called Michael who was intent on saving the world, a sister-in-law called Crissie who cared for him a lot more than she'd ever admit, and two of the nicest dogs I'd ever met. Oh, and he'd turned me on for the first time since Perry Fotheringay had so carelessly turned me off.

In other words he was a man to be avoided at all costs, because I certainly wasn't going to fall for that 'trust me...I'm a doctor' routine. He was a man, wasn't he? I'd had ample evidence of that while I'd been up close and personal. His mind was willing. It was just my good fortune that he was too weak to do anything much about it at the moment.

He'd recover.

But then he was taking a pretty big chance on me,

too. He knew even less about me than I did about him. He certainly didn't know I was a TFB—temporarily without the TF, it was true, but nevertheless well endowed with my own income. All I had to do was convince my father that he couldn't use it to control me. Or get married. Or wait until I was thirty.

I could be a crook for all he knew and, having gained his confidence with my ministering angel routine, I could empty his house while he was asleep. Run off with his credit cards. Perpetrate fraud of all kinds.

I could even be a *dognapper*, for heaven's sake. I'd heard of that. People stealing precious pets and holding them to ransom…

Now *I* was the one hallucinating. Lost in the realms of fantasy. Or more likely just putting off the inevitable.

He was the one who was sick, and I knew I was going to worry about him every minute of the day while he was out of my sight. I did that. Worried about helpless things.

I mean, who was going to give the stripey cat kibbles now I was leaving Chandler's Reach? Who was going to give her that stuff that stopped fleas and all the other nasties?

No one. That was who.

But I could ensure that Gabriel York was taken care of. That he had something to eat. That someone would be around if he had another dizzy spell.

I could even phone Crissie and put her mind at ease.

Having convinced myself that I was doing the right thing, I didn't waste too much time packing. I just flung everything I was likely to need in the next couple of weeks into a suitcase, including my hot water bottle. Just in case Gabriel got the shivers again; I didn't think a repeat of the heat transfer treatment would be good for my peace of mind.

Then, because his fridge was bare, I filled a carrier with the contents of my own fridge. Flung in a few other essentials.

Finally I left a note, asking Nigel and Amber to pack up the rest of the stuff in my room and send it home to Berkshire. And the bill to my father. It was the least they could do under the circumstances. The least he could do. I finished by wishing them good luck in their new home. I meant it, too. My predicament wasn't their fault, after all.

I left my keys on the kitchen worktop, so that if I lost my nerve between Chelsea Harbour and Pimlico there could be no turning back. And Gabriel York's address with the porter so that he could forward my mail.

The taxi was halfway to Pimlico when I made the driver turn around and go back. The cat was pleased to see me, although she wasn't quite so happy about the taxi ride. She remembered the last time she'd been in one, probably. When she'd cut her paw and I'd taken her to the vet.

But I found a few kibbles in my pocket to distract her and I made it without too many scratches.

I dumped my bags and the cat in the spare bedroom, before fetching her a saucer of milk and finding her an old jumper to curl up on when she was finished—just so that she'd know she was in clover. Then I plugged in my mobile to recharge and, making sure to shut the door so that she couldn't escape, went to check on Gabriel.

He was fast asleep. He didn't seem to be feverish, but I made a hot water bottle just in case, and slipped it under the quilt at the bottom of the bed, then held my breath as he turned over. I didn't want to have to confess to the cat just yet. I needed time to think of a really good reason why I hadn't mentioned her before. When he'd suggested I move in.

I didn't want it to be *that* temporary.

Then I took the dogs out.

They didn't want to go. They wanted to go upstairs and investigate the interesting new scent of cat. But I was firm and they were obedient, mostly. Or maybe they knew the cat would keep until they got back.

I decided it might be a good idea to wear them out and gave them a real workout, telling them that I was making up for their curtailed exercise the night before.

It gave me more time to work on my cat story.

There wasn't enough time in the world, I decided. As it happened, I didn't have to beat about the bush when I owned up. When I got back, Gabriel was stretched out in one of the kitchen armchairs.

The cat was on his knee.

Mayhem ensued.

The dogs, keen to fling themselves on Gabriel, were stopped in their tracks by the cat who, panicked into action, dug her claws into his leg, bringing him to his feet, cursing inventively and clutching at his knee.

I made a grab for her but she backed off, arching her back and hissing furiously, and when Joe—

younger and stupider than Percy—decided to investigate, and stuck his nose too close for her liking, she slashed at him with claws fully extended.

He yelped and leaped back, banging against the table, sending the jug of flowers flying.

The cat, having made her feelings well and truly felt, dived beneath the armchair.

For a moment all that could be heard was the gentle trickle of water as it ran over the edge of the table and splashed onto the quarry tiled floor.

I cleared my throat.

'Hi,' I said brightly, and, going for the obvious, 'You're awake.'

I got a look that would have curdled milk. 'Your cat objected to being shut in. Loudly.'

'Did she?' All innocence. 'In clover' hadn't worked, then. 'I'm really sorry. She's not used to being shut up.'

'That would be why she was trying to claw her way through the door, I expect.'

Pure sarcasm. This was definitely not the moment to reveal that she wasn't used to being inside, let alone shut up. 'Oh, your poor leg!' I exclaimed, hoping to distract him with the trickle of blood that had appeared beneath the hem of his bathrobe. 'You should put something on it. Have you got any antiseptic?'

Gabriel gave me a look that warned me he knew exactly what I was doing and he hadn't finished with the subject, but for the moment he left it. 'There might be some in the cupboard under the sink.'

There was. I poured some into a bowl and diluted it, then, lacking cotton wool, I further demonstrated my ability for improvisation by dipping the end of my T-shirt into the bowl.

As I turned to demonstrate, yet again, that I was a dab hand at first aid, he said, 'You can't use that!'

'Don't make such a fuss. It's clean.'

'But is it sterilised?'

'Have you got an unopened pack of cotton wool?' I demanded. His only response was to glare at me. 'No, I thought not.' He might be a doctor, but I was in no mood to take any namby-pamby nonsense from Gabriel York. 'Just sit down and let me clean you up.'

Maybe he recognised that argument was futile. Or maybe he wasn't feeling strong enough to follow through. Whatever, he subsided into the armchair and, since I had no wish to renew my acquaintance with his sexy underwear—assuming he was still wearing underwear—I carefully lifted aside his bathrobe and blotted his knee.

'Will I live?' he enquired, sounding as if he didn't much care one way or the other.

'I can't guarantee it,' I said, concentrating on cleaning up the rest of his leg. 'Not unless you eat something very soon. An egg would be good.' If I was going to browbeat him into eating some breakfast I might as well make it worth my while. There was no immediate response to this and I looked up. 'Any time in the next half an hour,' I prompted.

'I told you that I'm not looking for a nurse,' he said, not in the least bit amused. Clearly he was having second thoughts about his rash invitation for me to move in. 'I seem to recall receiving an assurance that I wasn't getting one.' Okay, third thoughts. Or possibly even fourth ones.

'You did,' I assured him, equally straight-faced. 'I lied.'

I was hoping that might raise the promise of a smile, but in case it didn't I got quickly to my feet and crossed to where the dogs had prudently re-treated, to the safety of the far side of the kitchen, and repeated my first aid on poor Joe's nose. That sensible creature raised no objections to my T-shirt. Just whimpered for a cuddle.

He got one. As did Percy.

'I don't recall you mentioning a cat, either,' Gabriel said, interrupting this canine love-in. 'Didn't it occur to you that she might not want to share a kitchen with two dogs?'

'She hasn't got a choice. It's their kitchen.' I finally turned to face him. 'I couldn't leave her behind, Gabriel.'

'I didn't suggest you could. But you should have told me. Have you any idea of the noise that creature was making?'

I considered, briefly, what it must have been like waking up to the yowling of a desperate cat; I was well aware of how much noise she could make. I was rather more concerned at the kind of mess she'd made…

'Yes, I should. I'm sorry. I hoped she'd settle down and sleep for an hour while I walked the dogs. If you want to withdraw your invitation, I'll quite under-stand.'

'Where would you go?'

Damn! He wasn't supposed to say that! He was

supposed to say that of course he wouldn't do any such thing. That they'd quickly sort out territorial boundaries and settle down. Which they would. Probably.

On the other hand, I could sympathise with his point of view. Bringing the cat was undoubtedly taking advantage of his generosity.

'I suppose I'd have to give in and go home,' I said.

Choice one—Tony—was now a complete non-starter. He was allergic to cats. And I'd left the keys behind to prevent a bolt back to safety. Maybe my subconscious had been busily burning all bridges behind me when it had prompted me to go back for her. I wanted to stay here...

'Where's home?'

'What? Oh, Berkshire. It's a bit too far to come and walk your dogs twice a day.' When he didn't respond to that prompt, I added, 'I'm afraid I'd have to charge travelling expenses.'

Oh, oh... nearly got him with that one.

'That's a consideration,' he said carefully. Damn it, smile! It won't kill you... 'And then, of course, there's your job at the flower shop. There'd be no one to clean that.'

'Well, quite.'

There was a long moment when he appeared to be considering it, before he did something with his shoulders that was very nearly a shrug. Something with his mouth that was very nearly a smile.

'Why don't you show me how good you are with scrambled eggs?' he finally invited. 'Then I'll decide.'

Which effectively took my mind off the problem

of the cat. Of all the egg dishes in all the world he had to choose to have his scrambled...

Not good.

But not bad either.

From beneath his armchair I could hear the cat purring contentedly, and, to be honest, I felt a bit like purring myself.

Gabriel had more or less promised to eat something nourishing. And I had somewhere to live while I sorted myself out.

All I had to do was scramble an egg without burning it.

There was a first time for everything.

'I'll, um, just go and wash my hands.'

'Don't be long.'

I must have looked as surprised as I felt. I hadn't got any real feeling that he was panting for breakfast.

'You said I had half an hour,' he reminded me.

'Yes, but I was only—'

'Joking?'

Don't you just hate men who can keep a poker-straight face even when they're teasing?

'Only offering a rough estimate,' I countered. 'Who knows? You may have as long as an hour.' If I didn't kill him first. I was beginning to see where Crissie was coming from...

I tugged off my soggy, antiseptic-soaked top and gave my hands a scrub—I didn't anticipate that he'd have any real appetite for my scrambled eggs, but if they tasted of antiseptic it was quite possible that he'd never eat again.

I dug around in my suitcase, found a fresh T-shirt, then picked up my mobile and switched it on. It beeped to let me know I had messages. I turned it back off. They would have to keep. Right now I had something more important on my mind.

Scrambled eggs.

The last thing I needed was Miss Frosty phoning me and disturbing my concentration. I already had one brooding presence in the corner to do that.

'Okay. To work,' I said brightly, looking around the kitchen in an attempt to get my bearings. It wasn't exactly the kind of kitchen that would have lifestyle magazines clamouring for a photo-shoot, but it had possibilities.

There was a terrific butler sink. A huge old Welsh dresser minus the fancy china—just piled up with books and papers, all of them coated with a fine film of dust. I was overcome with an unexpected urge to find a duster and do something about it.

I managed to restrain myself.

One of the walls was completely filled with fitted cupboards and drawers, as if someone had embarked on a Shaker-style upgrade but had lost interest before completing the job. No self-respecting Shaker would allow that disreputable old sofa, and the mismatched armchairs in her kitchen.

Then there was the big wooden table, the only work surface, dominating the business end of the room. I mopped up the spilt water and topped up the jug.

'Are they perks of the job?' Gabriel asked. 'The flowers?'

'Pretty, aren't they?' I set the jug on the windows-ill, tidied the dishevelled posy. 'They were up to their armpits at Bloomers last night, working on big wed-ding.' I straightened the posy, touched a blushing pink rosebud. The bride would be awake now, too excited to sleep, too nervous for breakfast, her designer gown waiting under its covers. The man of her dreams ready to commit himself for the rest of his life... 'These were just a few discarded scraps.'

'And the roses and orchids and sunflowers?'

'What?' I turned to look at him. 'Oh, those.' I'd put them in my bedroom. He must have seen them when he'd let the cat out. 'No. They aren't perks of the job. It was my birthday a couple of days ago.'

'And you got flowers? Isn't that a bit like sending coal to Newcastle?'

'I only started at the flower shop yesterday.' I didn't want to discuss my lack of a career plan with Gabriel York, so I opened the nearest cupboard and found not bowls, or pans, or anything seriously useful, just a stack of medical journals. Great. 'Look, if I'm working against the clock, you're going to have to help me out here. I need a bowl. I need a whisk. I need a saucepan. A non-stick saucepan,' I added hastily. Then I gestured at the array of cupboards. 'Would you care to give me a clue?'

'Sorry, I haven't any idea where things are kept.'

Of course not. He was a man. He sat back and let someone else cook for him.

Who? Someone he'd hurt as she'd been brushed aside in the slip-stream? The nurse who'd cared for his dogs...?

I felt a totally unexpected, unlooked-for riffle of jealousy sweep through me at the thought of some unknown woman in his kitchen. Cooking. And wished I'd spent a little of the past twenty-five years learning how to cook proper food.

A man couldn't live on fairy cakes and scones…

'In that case,' I said, 'this may take some time.'

'I have no pressing engagements.'

There was something in his voice that made me turn. His hands were caught in tight fists, his expression bleak, and I had the feeling that he'd been making an effort just for me.

As if aware that he'd betrayed himself in some way, he forced a rictus smile that chilled my heart.

That was *so* not the kind of smile of I'd hoped for.

'That makes two of us,' I said, pretending that I hadn't noticed anything odd. I began to work my way through the cupboards, finally running to earth everything I needed, then made a start on unpacking the groceries I'd brought with me, putting them away in the fridge. Apart from the eggs. I'd need them. The box seemed a bit light and I opened it to discover that it contained only two eggs. Thank you, Nigel and Amber. I hope you enjoyed your breakfast before you left…

But the bread was okay for toast and the butter was fresh.

It had seemed to take for ever to assemble the equipment, but finally I was done. Then I looked for a toaster. There wasn't one. Great. That meant I was going to have to watch the toast *and* the eggs. At the same time.

The tension between the livestock didn't exactly help. Joe had recovered his courage and was inching across the floor on all fours towards the armchair. I had the uneasy feeling that total warfare was going to break out the moment I took my eye off him.

'Joe! Stay.' I turned as Gabriel warned the dog. Joe

sat up, a big daft smile on his face. All innocence. Gabriel placed his hand on the dog's head to reward his obedience and I had a flash image of a prince sitting on his throne, faithful hound at his side.

I needed to get more sleep.

'Shall I turn up the heating?' He didn't answer. 'You're shivering, Gabriel. Is it the fever...?'

I was looking at his hands, and he clenched them to stop the tremor. 'No. It's not the fever. It's nothing heat will cure.'

And then I was the one with a streak of ice racing down my spine. He was a surgeon. An eye surgeon. With a tremor. And I thought I had problems.

I wanted to put my arms around him and hold him and tell him it would be all right. That it was only temporary. His expression warned me that I couldn't promise that. That the perfect steadiness of the hand, once lost, might never be regained...

'You need to eat,' I said, sounding exactly like my mother faced with a crisis. 'It won't be long.' And I began to beat the eggs furiously.

I put the bread under the grill and the eggs on a low heat, but it was a slow business. I had to take them off the heat while I looked at the toast. And I didn't dare leave the toast. I had to get this right. It was important.

'Here, let me do that.'

The grill pan hit the floor as he placed his hand on my shoulder. The dogs flew onto the sofa, flattening their long, elegant heads as close to the cushions as possible. The cat's tail lashed angrily from beneath the chair.

'Damn it!' I turned on him. 'You made me jump!'

'Sorry.' He picked up the grill pan and slid it back under the heat. 'It's just that you looked a little stressed.'

'That could be the understatement of the year. This domestic goddess stuff is all new to me.'

'I had noticed.'

'No, Gabriel, you're supposed to say that since I'm a goddess you can manage without the domesticity,' I snapped. Then, realising I'd overreacted just a little bit, 'However, you're sick, so I'll forgive you. This time.'

'You're a goddess?' He sounded sceptical. 'Is that the kind of response you usually evoke in the male breast?'

I reached up and put my hand on his forehead. 'Cool, dry... Extraordinary. I thought you must be running a raging temperature to have asked a fool question like that.' Then, suddenly self-conscious as I realised what I'd done, I took my hand away, curling my fingers against my palm. 'Of course, you haven't seen me at my best.'

'No?' He smiled. He actually smiled. 'I thought you were pretty amazing, actually. Not a goddess, but pretty amazing nonetheless. But if there's more...'

Oh, good grief. I could see why he didn't do it often. The smile. I'd always known it was going to be special, but that was understatement on a grand scale. It should have a health warning attached.

Danger: this smile is bad for your heart...

Mine responded by putting in a couple of little skips that threw it completely out of sync. And left me totally speechless.

'Shall I keep an eye on the toast?' he asked finally.

'Um…'

My brain had seized up, too.

'One of us should, or it'll burn…'

I went to snatch it from the heat, but he beat me to it. Turned it over.

'Why don't you take care of the eggs?' he suggested.

'Right,' I said. 'Good plan.'

Maybe in the end it was a good thing it had taken such an age to prepare. That I was so useless that he'd had to get involved. There was nothing like the scent of warm toast to tempt a jaded appetite. Nothing like waiting to make you long to sink your teeth into it. And Gabriel ate every scrap of the meagre spoonful of egg—which was absolutely perfect, even if I do say so myself—resting on the single slice of lightly buttered toast. Equally perfect.

We made a good team.

I would have given him all of the egg, but I knew that if I didn't have anything he'd make a fuss. I wasn't about to give him any excuse to duck out of eating what I'd sweated over, and I knew it would be better to leave him wanting more than pushing away what he couldn't eat.

Of course he might just have made the effort to eat because it had obviously been such an effort for me to prepare the food. I didn't care. He'd eaten something that I'd cooked for him and I felt triumphant. Ready to tackle chicken soup—although I knew better than to say so.

And first I'd need a recipe.

I was still starving, of course.

'Would you like some tea?' I offered as I gathered

the plates to cover the sound of my stomach rumbling. There was cottage cheese in the fridge, but that wasn't going to help. This wasn't a cottage cheese sort of week. I'd grab a burger when I was out; I was burning up calories by the thousand, okay? And possibly some fries. 'I've got some Earl Grey.' I would have preferred coffee—a double espresso would have been about perfect—but I can't stand coffee when I'm off-colour. Even the smell...

'No. Thanks. I'll stick to water.'

'Look, maybe you should go back to bed,' I suggested. Good food and sleep. Nature's cure... I blinked. If my mother didn't come back soon I was going to turn into her.

'What are you going to do now?'

'Wash up?' I suggested.

'You said you had to look for a job.'

And somewhere to live, hint, hint.

'Wash up and then check my laptop and mobile to see what fabulous offers have been pouring in overnight,' I advanced, hoping he'd get the message that I wouldn't be under his feet for long.

'Why don't you work in the kitchen? It's warmer.' He got up and headed for the stairs.

'Gabriel...' He glanced back. 'Thank you.' I made a vague gesture that encompassed the cottage. 'This is a life-saver.'

'Then we're quits.'

I wasn't looking for any settling of imagined debts, simply grateful for the breathing space he'd given me to sort myself out, but I let it go. I waited until he'd used the bathroom and settled himself back in bed before I went upstairs to collect my laptop. I listened to my messages while I waited for it to boot up.

There were a lot of messages. Some of the people who'd been at my party, just to say 'great party' and 'what are we doing this weekend?'. Maybe it was reaching the advanced age of twenty-five, but suddenly filling the weekend with entertainment didn't feel like the most important thing in the world.

There was a message from my sister, who wanted to talk about Dad. In other words, when was I going to go home and take care of him...?

Three eager messages from Tony, offering me sanctuary, each one more fulsomely than the one before. I got the feeling that if I hung on long enough he'd offer to move out and let me have his apartment.

It occurred to me that I needed to take a step back. Give him a chance to meet someone who'd return his affection with more than—well, affection.

And finally there was one from Miss Frosty.

She had a job for me doing some shopping for an elderly lady. I checked in, took the details. I didn't, I noticed, get any sarcasm from her this time. Things were looking up.

The internet agency wanted to know if I wanted a job as a waitress in a pub. Now that I could do. From the age of twelve Kate and I had earned extra pocket money by laying the table and acting as waitresses at dinner parties for Mum.

I called the number and they wanted me *now*. Black trousers, white shirt; they'd provide the apron.

I tapped on Gabriel's door and he shouted for me to come in. He was propped up against the pillows, reading something weighty. He looked up as I stuck my head around the door.

'I've got a couple of jobs. I'm just going to get Tigger—' I'd thought a name might give the cat a little probity, but didn't have time to get inventive '—some kitty litter, then I'll be gone until about four-thirty. Have you got your mobile?' He indicated the bedside table. 'If you need me ring, okay? I don't want to come back to another crisis.'

'No, ma'am.'

'Don't mock. Are you warm enough? Do you want a fresh hot water bottle?'

'Stop clucking about me like some mother hen. I've had breakfast. Your good deed is done for the day.'

His phone lay on the bedside table and, ignoring this rapid reversion to bear-with-sore-head mode—for all I knew, he had a sore head—I said, 'You've still got my number?'

He picked it up and I thought for a moment that he was going to throw it at me. Instead he said, 'Remind me. I'll program it in.'

'Under G for goddess?'

'Under N for nag. There. Happy?' he asked when I'd refreshed his memory.

'Delirious,' I said.

'For all the good it will do me.'

'I'm fully charged,' I informed him. 'All you have to do is call.'

I was halfway down the mews when my phone rang. 'Sophie Harrington, universal aunt. No job too small,' I said.

'This hot water bottle…'

His voice, low, slightly gravelly, totally unexpected, brought a warm rush of some forgotten youthful joy surging through my body. I made a belated effort to dam it up, but without success. He'd got to me. And I couldn't even blame the smile. He'd got to me the minute I set eyes on him.

'What about the hot water bottle?' I enquired, cool as a cucumber. I might have lost all control of my emotions, but I was still in charge of my voice.

'It looks like a sheep.'

All street-cred blown, I confessed as much. 'His name is Sean.'

'Sean the Sheep?' Yes, that was disbelief in his gravelly voice.

'He's cuddly. And he's comforting.'

In other words, about as unlike Gabriel York as it was possible to get.

'If I need to be cuddled or comforted, I'll let you know. And in the meantime please take note that if I need emergency warming I don't want this sheep as a stand-in. I want the heat transfer method.'

Maybe his tremor was catching, because without warning I was standing in the middle of the cobbled mews and my whole body was trembling. But, since it would be total madness to do what it was telling me to do—rush back and jump right in beside him—I said, 'C-call a plumber.'

The stutter undermined my throw-away attempt to make light of it. But that was okay. He didn't hear me.

I was already listening to the dialling tone.

CHAPTER SEVEN

'SOPHIE?'

'Oh, hi, Kate. I didn't think you were back until tomorrow. How was Scotland?'

'Forget Scotland. How are *you*?'

'Me? I'm fine.' More than fine. Great.

'More to the point, where are you? I just called round to the flat to see you and Amber told me they've bought the flat. That you've moved out.'

'I was going to call you.' Tomorrow... 'Cora needed the money.'

'And she asked you to move out without any notice? How could she do that?'

'With great embarrassment. She's been good to us, Kate. I didn't want to make it any tougher for her. Don't worry; I've got somewhere to stay while I sort myself out.'

'With Tony? Is that wise? You know how he dotes on you—'

'Not Tony. It's no one you know. But if you hear of anything—'

'For heaven's sake, Sophie, why don't you just do us all a favour and go home for a while?'

I stared at the phone.

'Dad called last night. I'm sure he'd been drinking. I tried talking to Mum, but she refused to discuss it. Please, Sophie. I can't take any more time off work.'

And I didn't have a job. Not a proper one. She

122

wouldn't be impressed with the dog-walking, or shopping for the housebound, or cleaning, or the late-night shelf stacking at the toy store.

'And Simon needs me,' she added.

Or a life.

'I can't right now. I have commitments, too.'

She made a dismissive little noise that I found distinctly annoying. My commitments might not pay as much as hers, but they were no less important—and Christmas was getting closer. Even those of us without a life still had cards and gifts to buy...

'Couldn't you at least go down at the weekend?' she said.

'I don't have a car, Kate.'

Gabriel did, though. A big silver Range Rover with plenty of room for two dogs in the back. He'd been convalescing for nearly two weeks now. A walk in the country would do him good.

'The problem with a portfolio career—' and I was building up an impressive portfolio of 'little' jobs '—is that it doesn't leave a lot of time for flat-hunting.'

'You don't have a career, Sophie,' Gabriel said from behind the Sunday newspaper. 'You're just a general dogsbody, gofer and dog-walker.'

'I'm fulfilling a need.' I applied a little more beeswax to the dresser. 'Take Mrs Andrews, for instance.'

'Must I?'

'She's the lady I shop for each morning.'

'I imagine she pays you handsomely for the service?'

'Yes, of course she does.' Then, 'Well, not handsomely, but probably more than she can afford. I could do it once a week, and clearly it would be a lot cheaper for her, but that's my point. It isn't shopping she needs; it's someone to talk to. She's always got a pot of coffee waiting when I get back, and some little treat. In fact I think she just buys the biscuits and cake especially for me. What do I do? Say, Sorry, too busy...?' Encouraged by the lack of a reply, I continued, 'We have coffee and cake and she tells me all about her life. She was a musician. A violinist. She travelled all over the world with her orchestra, met some amazing people.'

'You're not supposed to stay and chat, Sophie. You don't get paid for that.'

'You're totally heartless.'

'That, as you must know, is a physiological impossibility.'

'I was speaking figuratively, Doctor,' I replied, gallantly resisting this open invitation to inform him that he was a miserable pedant. 'Your heart is nothing more than an emotionally sterile pump. It beats, but it doesn't...*feel*.'

'Doctors can't afford to be emotional. Neither can a girl who hasn't got a proper job.'

'She's lonely, Gabriel.'

'She should get a cat.' He glanced over the top of the newspaper. 'Why don't you give her yours?'

'Very funny.'

'I was perfectly serious. This woman—'

'She has a name.'

'—is keeping you from earning a living.' He didn't say...and finding somewhere to live. He didn't have to.

'It's not her fault.'

I'd been staying with Gabriel for nearly two weeks and so far hadn't done a thing about finding somewhere else. I was attempting to explain why. It wasn't that I didn't intend looking. Every day I set out with the best of intentions. I just never seemed to have the time to do anything about them.

'Every minute of my day seems to be taken up with rushing from one job to the next.'

'I'd have thought it would give you more freedom,' he said, manfully resisting the open invitation to remind me that I could have spent the time I was wasting chatting to Mrs Andrews rather more usefully in the pursuit of suitable accommodation.

'Theoretically,' I admitted, 'it does. In practice it just doesn't seem to work out that way.' Especially since I was going out of my way to call back at the mews two or three times a day to make sure he was okay. 'I've asked everyone I know to keep an eye out for me, though,' I said, rubbing at a particularly stubborn mark.

'Good. Let's hope they have twenty-twenty vision.'

'I just didn't want you to think I'm taking advantage of your good nature.'

'I don't have a good nature. Ask anyone who knows me.'

'I know you, and I'm telling you that your nature is perfectly good. You took me in when I was pretty desperate—'

He finally gave up trying to read the paper. 'What the hell are you doing?'

It was a classic diversionary tactic, but I let him get away with it. For now. 'Getting rid of some dust,' I said.

The dark wood of the Welsh dresser gleamed in the low winter sunlight that had finally reappeared after days of drizzle and gloom. It was the sunlight that had driven me into action, showing up the layers of dust, every mark and smear.

'Stirring it up and moving it around, more like,' he said. 'It'll get in your bronchial tubes and irritate them. Worse, it'll get in mine.'

'You don't need dust to irritate you. It's your natural state.'

'Proving my point that I don't have a good nature and that you're living dangerously—'

'I've been doing that since I knocked on your door,' I reminded him. I'd started out determined to keep my cool—I had an ulterior motive for this conversation—but I was only human and my own irritability quotient was ratcheting up with every exchange.

There was a momentary pause before he said, 'A little dust, left undisturbed, won't harm you. Best leave well alone.'

Easier said than done.

'This from the man who objected to the fact that my T-shirt hadn't been sterilised when I cleaned up a scratch on his knee?'

He responded with something that sounded distinctly nineteenth century. 'Pshaw', perhaps. Or maybe it was nearer 'harrumph'. Or it might have been altogether less polite. And retreated behind the newspaper.

'How is it now? Your knee?' I enquired, with saccharine sweetness. 'Any sign of infection?' He muttered something unintelligible. 'Sorry? I didn't quite catch that.'

'It's fine. What's for breakfast?'

I wasn't fooled by this sudden change of subject. I was doing my very limited best to produce the kind of light but tasty food to tempt his appetite, but he wasn't eating enough to keep a bird alive. That was, I fully admit, probably as much to do with my cooking as his lack of interest in food. The scrambled eggs had been a high point that I hadn't managed to repeat.

And, like his appetite, his temper was deteriorating with every passing day.

The promising moment of closeness, of teasing intimacy, as he'd invited me to be his personal body-warmer hadn't lasted beyond the telephone call. Maybe I should have turned around and gone back then. By the time I'd shopped for Mrs Andrews and spent two hours waiting on lunchtime tables—they'd been really desperate at the pub, so my interview had involved tying on an apron and getting on with it— he'd been back to high-octane grouch mode.

He hadn't wanted to eat; he hadn't wanted anything except to be left alone. And he hadn't cavilled at telling me so.

In fact he couldn't have made it plainer that he was sorry he'd invited me and my cat to stay.

Well, just me. He hadn't invited the cat, obviously.

Tough. He was stuck with us until he was well enough to be left on his own or until I could find somewhere I could afford. Of the two, the former was more important. But I didn't tell him that. Or that I was ringing Crissie every day to keep her up to date with his progress.

Nil.

Not that he was malingering in bed. Making a performance out of being an invalid. I wished he *would* stay in bed, instead of pacing feverishly, reading great tomes of text books. He needed to rest.

I'd only suggested it once, and had my head bitten off for my trouble. So, since I was tired of asking him what he'd like to eat and being told to leave him in peace, that if he wanted anything from me he'd say so, I'd made him a cup of tea and left him to his newspaper while I got on with cleaning the dresser. Right now he was using it as a barrier between us, holding it up so that I couldn't see his face. As I stood there it began to shiver like an aspen leaf, and with an exclamation of annoyance he tossed it aside.

'I don't know why I waste my time reading this rubbish,' he declared furiously, standing up as if he wanted to run and run…but knew there was nowhere to hide. He looked thinner, paler, his dark eyes hot and angry at his helplessness. And my heart, my poor heart that had never been disturbed by anyone since Perry Fotheringay had broken it, was hit by a shockwave of an emotion so strong that I was rocked to my heels. Had to clutch at the dresser for support.

I yearned to reach out, take his shaking hand in mine and hold it to my breast, heal him with my warmth. Even as I moved to make the thought the deed I was repelled by the force field of keep-your-distance anger with which he'd surrounded himself; I suspected that it was the only thing holding him together. I recognised the symptoms. I'd been there.

Oh, I hadn't used anger to hide my hurt. I'd used careless gaiety—cut myself off from all risk of emotional attachment with an endless round of parties and shopping and meaningless jobs.

How shallow it was. How stupid. What overweening self-pity and pride to think that my eighteen-year-old heart was worth so much.

What was a broken heart compared to the prospect of never being able to use his hands to repair, heal, restore the precious gift of sight...?

Nothing.

I would have done anything to spare him that. Anything to ease the pain just a little. Given him the one gift a woman could offer to help a man forget everything, lose himself for just a few moments. But I knew he'd see it as an act of pity and loathe the weakness in himself that had evoked it. Loathe me for seeing him so reduced.

I wasn't sure whether the keep-your-distance snapping was to prevent me from getting close enough to hold him in the simple act of comfort or to prevent himself from reaching out and accepting it.

I'd thought I was good at concealing my feelings, but perhaps the feelings were too strong to hide and my face betrayed me, because he turned the anger on me. 'Well?' he demanded. 'What does a man have to do around here to get some breakfast?'

Good move. Great distraction. I wasn't falling for it.

'Ask nicely?' I suggested. If I couldn't use desire to promote a little temporary amnesia, I'd use whatever emotion came to hand. 'Or get it himself.'

His response was to cross to the fridge and take out a new carton of orange juice. I knew from experience that they were a pig to open, but knew better than to offer to do it for him. By the time he'd managed to tear an opening his hand was shaking so badly that he spilled more than he poured into the glass. He stared at the mess for a moment, then picked up the glass and threw it hard at the nearest wall. I flinched as it smashed in a shower of splintered glass and juice.

No emotion, huh?

Into the ghastly silence, during which the juice—it was the thick kind, full of pulp—slithered down the wall, I said, 'There is a third alternative.'

He turned a ferocious glare on me, taking a step towards me as if he wanted to take me by the shoulders and shake me. I bet he'd reduced junior doctors and nervous young nurses to jelly with that performance. I stood my ground. If he wanted to do that to me, he was using the wrong technique. He should try the smile…

'Well, don't keep me in suspense,' he snapped, belatedly remembering to keep his distance. I didn't want him to remember. I wanted him to forget. Everything. Once he'd touched me, once I had him in my arms, anything might be possible…

'You could take me to that little Italian place on the corner.'

His eyes flared. 'Why should I do that?'

'Because I've walked your dogs and polished your dresser and now I'm hungry.'

'I pay you to walk my dogs. Extra on Sundays,' he reminded me, and I couldn't fault him. 'And I didn't ask you to polish anything.' He seemed impregnable, but he wasn't. I knew he felt something. Knew he wanted to touch me, wanted to hold me. I'd been there in his bed…

'It's breakfast, for heaven's sake, not dinner at the Ritz. I'm hungry, I don't feel like cooking, and…and I hate going into strange places on my own.' Maybe that was a step too far. 'Also,' I declared, 'you could do with some fresh air—'

'It's not fresh; it's freezing. I'll get pneumonia.'

'Wimp,' I said. 'The sun's shining, for heaven's sake. It'll give you an appetite. And the food will be edible.'

'Well, that's a plus,' he conceded. With sarcasm like that, I decided, he didn't need a scalpel.

'Also, you've been a Grade A grouch all week,' I continued, on a roll. I knew I should clear up the glass before one of the dogs decided that it was safe to get down off the sofa and investigate, but Gabriel was talking, reacting—angrily, but reacting—and I wasn't going to give up while there was a chance that he'd crack, just a little… 'I deserve a break.'

'Grouch? I'm not a grouch. I've been the very soul of patience,' he ground out. 'Tolerant beyond belief, considering I haven't had a moment's peace with you rushing in and out all day. Your phone ringing non-stop. Considering,' he added, getting into his stride, 'that you introduced a cat into my household without so much as a—'

'And,' I said, cutting him off in full flow. We were discussing his failings, not mine. 'I've been so busy working that I haven't had time to shop, so there's no bread.'

'You couldn't fit it in during your daily shopping trips for Mrs Andrews?' he enquired.

'She was paying for my time,' I reminded him, doing my best to try his patience and tolerance to the limit. 'You weren't.'

I could keep this up as long as he could.

'Are you saying that I have to buy an hour of your time to get some breakfast?' he demanded, taking another step towards me. I noticed the shaking had stopped.

'No. I'm saying you should wrap up warm and take me out to breakfast. I could murder a toasted muffin. One that isn't burnt.'

He didn't appear to have an answer to that one. Another minute and he'd remember he wasn't really hungry, that he was just mad at me, and retreat back into his shell of misery, so I did the big sigh thing, threw up my hands and said, '*Okay.* If you're going to be cheap, I'll split the bill with you. But that's the best offer you're going to get, so you'd—'

'Sophie...' Suddenly he was a lot closer.

'—better take it—'

He grabbed my shoulders. 'Sophie, shut up.'

'—while you—'

His mouth came down on mine, hard and hot. As kisses went, it certainly wasn't out of the fairytale school of romance, but what it lacked in tender finesse it more than made up for in fierce, breath-stopping intensity, and my crushed lips sizzled beneath his, the heat spreading in an arc of fire that threatened to consume my entire body.

It was swift, shocking, and all but overwhelming. I slammed my eyes shut and held on, doing my best to ignore the racketing demands of a hot, insane desire that seized me by the throat. It didn't mean any-

thing, I told myself. I'd pushed him over the edge—
it had been my firm intention to push him over the
edge—and I'd succeeded beyond my wildest dreams.
All I had to do was hang on to that thought and it
would be over in a moment…

Then his mouth softened.

Without warning his desperation to shut me up,
stop me nagging at him, had turned to something
quite different and I was in trouble.

His grip on my shoulders shifted, his fingers
spreading across my back, setting up ripples of sensual excitement that escalated all the need to be held,
loved, that I'd kept locked tightly away for so long.
I'd forgotten how it could take and possess you.

My body yielded to the demands of his mouth. My
lips parted, my tongue invited deeper exploration of
possibilities that for years my heart had denied. My
legs buckled and I swayed towards him, wanting to
feel his body against mine, the urgency of his need…

And then, just as suddenly, it was over.

'Is that it?' Gabriel demanded, his eyes hot, obsid-
ian-black. I would have taken a step back, except that
his fingers were still digging into my shoulders. 'Are
you quite finished?'

If I'd wanted to speak, I couldn't.

I swallowed, trying to recapture the flippant, dare-
you provocation that he'd cut off so effectively with
his mouth.

I'd provoked and, finally, he'd dared.

Good job, Sophie. Terrific job…

Except I'd been so determined to get through to
him I hadn't seen the danger. That in applying the

blowtorch to his emotional freeze-up I would, inevitably, be caught in the flame.

I hadn't been kissed like that since…

No. Forget 'since'. I'd never been kissed like that. Never felt like that. Shaken, stirred, to the very tips of my toes.

'Don't tell me I've finally managed to shut you up?'

I had to speak. Now. Had to act as if that was all he'd done. But it took every ounce of will-power to resist the desperate need to swallow before I said, 'That depends.'

I heard the words: sharp, couldn't-care-less. It didn't sound like my voice. And why, when I was shaking everywhere else, was my voice steady as a rock?

'Are you determined to stay here and mope, Gabriel? Or are you going to admit defeat? Prove that you can walk a hundred yards without falling flat on your face?'

His grip on my shoulders relaxed and then he let go. I felt adrift, alone.

'Will I get any peace until I agree?' he asked.

'What do you think?'

'I think a dose of fresh air suddenly seems very attractive. I'll get my coat.'

He turned and walked quickly away from me, and as I heard his feet pounding up the stairs I finally slumped against the dresser. Who knows how long I'd have stayed there if Joe—stupid, adorable Joe—hadn't slithered off the sofa, in that belly-to-the-ground way that dogs have when they hope not to be noticed, quite unable to resist the lure of the orange juice?

I called him off, sent him back to the sofa and, by the time Gabriel returned with his coat, I'd cleaned up glass and was back in control. Almost.

The chill put some colour into Gabriel's cheeks. I'd had a momentary qualm about dragging him out against his will, but eased my conscience by reminding myself that I was doing it for his own good, tucking my arm through his as if it was the most natural thing in the world. If he suspected it was just in case the effort was too much for him he didn't say so, but took my hand and eased my arm more firmly in place, so that I was close enough to feel his warmth.

He stopped and I looked up at him. 'Are you okay?'

'Yes. No. You engineered that, didn't you?'

'What?'

'Don't pull that stupid blonde stuff on me, Sophie. I've shared a house with you for nearly two weeks. You engineered that row—pushed me until I did what I've been wanting to do since you gave me the kiss of life.'

'Excuse me? I thought you said…' I stopped. That searing kiss? He'd been holding onto that for the best part of two weeks? But that meant…that meant… Actually, I wasn't sure what it meant. He fancied me rotten but didn't like me enough to bother getting involved? He fancied me rotten but liked me too much to risk getting involved, considering his family's apparent genetic inability to make an emotional commitment? He just fancied me… 'Um, you said…'

'I know what I said and I was right. It wasn't CPR, but I know how it made me feel. Alive.'

'Well…good.'

Except that it wasn't good. Not from his point of view. He didn't do relationships.

We were standing facing each other, our arms still linked, my hand on the soft cloth of his overcoat, my cheek almost brushing his lapel.

'Do you have a problem with that, Gabriel?' I asked, pushing for an answer. 'Feeling alive?'

He reached out, as if to touch my cheek, but thought better of it, curling his fingers back into his palm. Then he said, 'Good grief, is that a Christmas tree?'

What?

He was glaring at a window, ablaze with coloured lights, as if it was a personal affront. 'It's nowhere near Christmas.

He'd seized the first distraction that came to him— anything rather than confront the question. Discussion over. Change subject before it could get messy…

Too late. Life is messy, but it's the only one we have, and while you're trying to avoid pain—or trying avoid causing it—time doesn't stop. He'd lowered his guard, given me a taste of the passion he had battened down for fear of hurting someone in his driven need to be the best. Well, I was ready to take that risk, but for the moment I was happy to drop the subject. Just for now.

'Of course it's a Christmas tree. Where have you been for the last month?' I asked him as we resumed our stroll towards the coffee shop. Then, realising what I'd said, I apologised, 'Sorry, Gabriel, please forget I asked that question, but it *is* the middle of December. There are only eight shopping days to Christmas. We're rushed off our feet doing Christmas lunches for office parties at the pub. Turkey, mince pies and seasonal indiscretion—all to the accompaniment of ''White Christmas'' non-stop on the sound system.'

'That sounds like something to be missed.'

'Don't be such a misery. It's great to see people enjoying themselves. And the tips are great.'

'By the time Christmas arrives you'll be heartily sick of the whole thing,' he warned me, seizing this opportunity to steer the conversation well away from dangerous emotional currents.

'No. I love Christmas. It's always the same. The decorations, the cheesy songs on the radio, choosing the perfect presents.'

Even as I was saying the words I realised that this year nothing would be the same. Not keen to dwell on exactly what Christmas would be like this year, I turned and looked up at him. 'What about you? Have you got any plans? Will your brother and his wife be home by then? Or do you spend it with your parents?'

I was fishing, of course. What I really meant was, Will you be spending it with the nurse? I hadn't seen anyone special, but that didn't mean there wasn't someone. I wasn't there all the time. A bowl of fruit had materialised one day while I was out. He'd said the woman who'd taken care of his dogs had called round with it.

My brain assured me that she'd be some solid retired nurse, who made a little money taking care of people's animals while they were away.

But my imagination offered an alternative reality in which she was sexy and gorgeous, a thoroughly modern woman who, like him, preferred to keep relationships on a strictly physical level. Who knew what treats she dropped in with while I was busy rushing around serving turkey and all the trimmings between twelve and two every day?

'I usually work through the holiday,' he said, not answering any of those questions. Or perhaps giving me more of an answer than he'd intended. 'I suppose you'll be at home in the bosom of your family?'

'Not this year.'

The big family Christmas wasn't going to happen without my mother to organise it. She masterminded the whole thing—cutting the tree, everyone going to church at midnight, rounding up anyone from the village with no one to share the holiday with, Dad carving the turkey, the stupid games…

Even Kate had said she wouldn't be there. I understood. She'd want to start making her own family traditions. But it just made the huge empty gap in the family harder to paper over.

'My parents split up a few months ago,' I said. 'My mother is spending Christmas in the sun with her toy boy. As you can imagine, it's put a bit of a dampener on the whole ho-ho-ho thing.'

'You could always spend the day with Mrs Andrews, listening to her stories.'

I knew I could rely on him not be 'sympathetic'.

'I'm sure it would be a lot more fun than rattling around the house while my father drowns his sorrows in Scotch. I wonder if she's going to be on her own?' I said as we reached the coffee bar.

'Since she pays you to do her shopping just so that she has someone to talk to, I imagine the chances of that are quite high.'

Pretty much my own thought. 'Maybe I should do something about that.'

'Maybe you should.' He unhooked his arm from mine and reached over my head to push open the door.

'Hey, Doc! We missed you. Where've you been?' The man behind the vast chrome espresso machine hurried out, beaming a welcome that immediately turned to concern as he shook Gabriel's hand. 'Nowhere that did you any good,' he said, without waiting for an answer. 'Sit, sit. I'll get Maria to make you one of her special *zabaglione*. It'll put you right back on your feet.'

Zabaglione? With eggs so lightly cooked they might be considered raw? This should be interesting...

'Thank you, Marco.' *Huh?* 'Ask her to leave out the alcohol, though. I'm on all kinds of medication.'

'Sure, Doc, you leave it to me.' He turned to me, his expression including me in his broad smile. 'And for your friend?'

'Marco, this is Sophie. She's taking care of the dogs until I'm fit.'

'Just the dogs?' With one lift of his expressive eyebrows he conveyed whole paragraphs of meaning. 'And who's taking care of you?'

'She's doing her best to do that, too. But, as she's just pointed out most forcefully, I'm not being terribly receptive.'

'The British reputation for understatement is safe in his hands,' I said.

'The Doc only cares about other people, eh, Sophie?' Marco said, as if we alone understood him. 'So, what would you like?'

'A toasted muffin, please. And a large cappuccino.'

'Make that two cappuccinos,' Gabriel said.

Marco brought us our coffee and lingered to invite us to join his family at the local church to see his daughter in the Nativity play on the Friday before Christmas.

'We'd be honoured to come,' Gabriel said. And, actually, I wasn't as surprised as I believe he'd meant me to be.

His presence demanded 'pronto' by his wife, Marco left us with the promise that our food would be with us in *'un momento'*.

'The Grinch at a Nativity play?' I teased.

'Will you come with me?' he asked.

'Thanks. I wouldn't miss it for the world.'

'Don't thank me. I'm not being kind. I'm being selfish,' he said, and sounded thoroughly disgusted with himself. But he didn't withdraw the invitation.

My turn to change the subject, I decided.

'I get the feeling you eat here on a regular basis. You're almost part of the family.'

Gabriel shrugged. 'I work long hours and I can't be bothered to cook.'

A young girl brought my muffin and some butter. Then she fetched Gabriel's *zabaglione*, shyly placing it in front of him. Gabriel said something to her in Italian and she giggled, then, after glancing at me, whispered something back to him.

He spoke Italian?

How…how…*un-English.*

How wonderful.

How shaming. What had I been doing all my life that I couldn't speak another language properly? I hadn't even bothered to enrol in a computer course, despite all those big promises I'd made to myself…

'Lucia has heard we're going to see her play. She wants to know if that means you're my girlfriend,' Gabriel said, distracting me. And without warning that errant smile was simmering just beneath the surface. Just the promise of it made my cheeks feel warm. My heart beat a little faster than usual. My lips heated up with the memory of his kiss.

I knew that feeling. I'd felt that way when Perry Fotheringay had looked at me. Dazzled, reckless, excited. And I knew all the other feelings that went with it. Misery when he hadn't called. Heartache when he'd betrayed me.

The ice-cold feeling inside as I'd pretended that it didn't matter. That I'd never taken him seriously.

I stared into the trap I'd set for myself. And fallen right into.

Just because he didn't flirt, or smile too easily, and guarded his emotions, I'd thought I was safe, but I wasn't. I was going to get hurt again, but at least this time I knew the score. And if I could show Gabriel that he was wrong, that emotional commitment had nothing to do with genetics and everything to do with heart… For that, I'd risk any amount of pain.

'I'm your friend,' I said lightly. 'The fact that I'm a girl makes no difference.'

He said something to her and she laughed, clearly

not taken in by this sleight of language, before skipping happily back to her papa.

Gabriel said nothing to me until I bit into the muffin, and when I had my mouth safely full he said, 'It does make a difference, you know.'

What made a difference? With my mouth full, all I could do was raise my eyebrows at him.

'Being a girl.' He took his time, tasted the sweet egg dish. 'If you'd been a man, driving me insane with your endless nagging, Sophie, I wouldn't have kissed you to shut you up.'

There's only one way to deal with a man who's scored a cheap point.

I took my time about finishing the piece of muffin, wiped my fingers on the napkin, finished my cappuccino.

Only then did I sit back and say, 'Gabriel?'

'Yes?'

'Can I borrow your car this afternoon?'

CHAPTER EIGHT

GABRIEL YORK had to be a lot sicker than I'd realised. He didn't even flinch. His only response to this outrageous request was to glance at me and ask, 'Do you have insurance?'

'Er, yes.' I was covered for everything, from a tractor to my father's BMW and anything else I drove, by the estate motor policy. Not that I had ever actually wanted to drive the tractor—well, not since I was about ten anyway—or was likely to be allowed to drive his precious saloon, despite my Advanced Driver's Certificate. This was something my father insisted on for everyone who drove his vehicles since it kept the insurance premiums down.

'Then help yourself. Just be careful how you reverse out of the garage; it's a bit tight.'

He wasn't even going to insist on doing that bit himself? What kind of man was he?

'I'll try not to do too much damage.'

'Since you're insured I'm not sweating.'

'Right.' Well, that had fallen flat. Tony had practically gibbered when I'd asked if I could borrow *his* car. Of course it was a hand-built Morgan; he'd been on a waiting list for three years before it was finally delivered. And I'd only been teasing. Only a fool would drive in London if she didn't have to. 'Don't you want to know where I'm going?'

143

'So long as you're back to walk the dogs, that's your business.'

'Actually, it's yours, too. I thought I might take Joe and Percy out into the country for a good run.'

'Where?'

Now he was interested. Obviously he cared more about his dogs than his car. He was a man with his priorities, if not his heart, in the right place. 'Home. I can check up on my father at the same time.'

'And with the excuse of the dogs and getting my car back he won't be able to talk you into staying to look after him?'

'Smart, aren't you?' I said, embarrassed to have been so obvious.

'He can't make you stay if you don't want to, Sophie.'

'Oh, he won't say a word. But he'll be *so* pathetic. He won't have shaved for a week, the fridge will be bare, he'll have no clean clothes...'

'Oh, I see.' He didn't even bother to hide his smile. 'It's that soft heart of yours that you don't trust.'

'Nothing of the kind,' I declared hotly. 'My heart is as tough as old boots. Kate—my big sister—has been nagging me about it, that's all.'

'I didn't know you had a sister. Does she live in London, too?'

'Yes, but she's been away.'

'Well, if she's back there's no reason why she shouldn't go and make sure he's all right. If she's so worried about him.'

Implying that I wasn't.

'I suggested that,' I said, doing my best to live up to the 'tough as old boots' boast. 'Unfortunately she has a cast-iron excuse. Unlike me, she applied herself to her lessons, went to university and graduated with an impressive degree in law, as a result of which she now has an equally impressive job.' I threw in a careless shrug. 'The rewards of hard work are never having to go home and pick up the pieces when your parents' marriage falls apart...'

The careless shrug didn't work, and I found myself in urgent need of a sniff.

Oh, sugar!

If I wasn't jolly careful I was going to cry. I hadn't cried in years. But, while I was prepared to accept that my mother needed a break, some excitement, I really, really wished she'd come home now—I searched my pocket for a tissue and blew my nose—and not just because my father was being such a pain in the *gluteus maximus*...

'It's Sunday. Most of the lawyers I know take Sunday off,' Gabriel said, ignoring my pathetic sniffle.

'That's true. But because she's not only clever, but seriously beautiful, she now has a totally fabulous husband to complete the set. Sunday is their one day together.'

'Is that just a touch of an inferiority complex showing?' Gabriel said, sounding a touch bored. And why wouldn't he? Who wanted to listen to a poor little rich girl whining on about her problems? Not that he knew I was rich. Well, I wasn't now, and wouldn't be until I reached the age of thirty or married—whichever came sooner.

'Actually, no,' I said, making a good attempt at

matching his boredom with the subject and topping it. 'I never wanted the degree or the fancy job.'

'What did you want?'

That was the problem with going over the top; it led you into dangerous conversational waters and suddenly there you were, way out of your depth and sinking fast.

Frantically treading water, I edged back from emotional exposure, got a grip and painted a smile on my face. 'To have fun. What else?' I asked brightly.

He did not look impressed by that, either, and, put baldly that way, I could see that it wasn't an impressive ambition.

'You consider walking dogs, cleaning, waiting on tables in a pub to earn a crust, *fun*?'

'To tell you the truth, it's a big improvement on some of the jobs I've had in the past. And I'm getting to meet some really extraordinary people. Greta, for instance, at the florist. She's bringing up two children single-handed after their father died. It must be so tough for her, but I've never heard her utter a word of complaint. And Alan at the toy store. He was a "special needs" kid and he was put into care because his parents didn't want him, but now he's working his way through university—'

'I'm sure they're all wonderful people. But it's not something you'll want to be doing in five or ten years' time, is it?'

'Having fun?' I asked, wilfully choosing to misunderstand.

'Swabbing floors in a flower shop,' he replied, as selectively deaf as his dogs, apparently, when it came to taking a hint and dropping a subject. 'I may be wrong, but it doesn't quite seem to go with the top-of-the-range laptop and cellphone, the designer label clothes—'

I opened my mouth to protest.

'Cutting out the labels doesn't change what they are, Sophie.'

He'd noticed?

'It makes me feel better about wearing them to work. But you're right, of course,' I said. 'I won't be doing that.' I gave him just long enough to look smug before I said, 'It's just temporary cover while the lady who normally does it is recuperating from minor surgery. I'll have to find something else after the holiday.'

'I'm almost afraid to ask what.'

'Well, I was thinking of enrolling on a computer course.'

This time he did flinch. 'No. Don't do that, Sophie.'

'Why not?'

'I've seen the trouble you get into just sending e-mails. The thought of you doing something that really mattered would keep me awake at nights.'

'That sound you just heard was my self-esteem hitting the floor.'

Making no attempt to retrieve it, soothe it, hand it back to me, he said, 'If you really need a job—'

'You think I'm doing this for fun…?'

Oops.

Actually, it was worth having my feet chopped from under me—metaphorically speaking—just to see him smile. It was a good job I was sitting down on all counts.

'There must be something else you can do?'

'Must there?' I asked. Smile time was over and we were back to the career plan. 'I had this conversation with a woman at my employment agency very recently. She's the person who offered me the job walking your dogs.'

Which left him with nowhere to go.

'I think what you need, Sophie, is a husband,' he said. And there was absolutely no doubt in my mind that he remembered me telling him something very similar and was enjoying the opportunity to return the lecture.

'I can't cook,' I reminded him.

'A rich husband,' he amended.

'Too bad the one I had picked out had other plans.' Oh, fiddle-di-dee. I *sooo* had not meant to say that. Or maybe I had. I'd never had any trouble keeping my failed career plan from anyone else. 'Anyway,' I said, quickly returning to the original subject of this conversation, 'I need to go home this afternoon and check that my father is at least going through the motions of daily life.'

'But you don't intend to linger, and if you take my dogs and car you'll have all the excuse you need to get away again?'

'You think I'm being mean?'

'Only you can answer that one. Are you?'

'He's been doing some serious arm-twisting to get me to go home and take care of things until my mother comes to her senses.' I didn't voice the fear that was at the back of my mind. That she might never come to her senses…

'You mean he's cut off your allowance? That's what this is all about? No money, nowhere to live…'

'Actually, the flat that I'd been staying in wasn't anything to do with him.' Or was it? Was it possible that Cora and my Dad were in cahoots? Using me to try and get my mother to see sense and come home? I shook my head in an effort to clear it. 'I'm not about to let him get away with emotional blackmail,' I said.

'And if he asked you nicely?'

'Thankfully there's no danger of that. Why do you think my mother's lying by a swimming pool in Cape Town instead of at home organising the Christmas festivities, making sure no one in the village is alone on the big day, that everyone is having a good time?'

'Maybe she thinks it's someone else's turn.'

'Thanks. Add selfish daughter to selfish husband and it's obvious why she left home.'

'I'm not criticising you, Sophie. He's an adult. Responsible for his own life. It's just that you don't seem particularly happy—'

'Yes, well, you can tell yourself that what you're doing is right, for the best, but when it comes right down to it…' I was avoiding looking at Gabriel '…well, he's still my dad.' I painted a smile on my face and looked up. 'I suppose you don't fancy coming with me?' I asked brightly, now that he'd given me the opening I'd been hoping for. 'It'll get you out of the house for a few hours.'

'You suppose correctly.'

I didn't push it. 'Okay, but if I'm not home by the dogs' bedtime you'd better send out a rescue party,' I said, hanging onto the smile by the skin of my teeth.

I couldn't believe how miserable I was that he'd turned me down.

'I'll ring you on that expensive cellphone at a pre-arranged time and get heavy about needing the car, if you like,' he offered.

'That's the best you can do?'

'I'd need a lot more to tempt me out than an hour's drive along the motorway followed by an uncomfortable confrontation with your father.'

'We could take the dogs for a walk in the woods. You should start getting some exercise.'

'Thanks for the consultation, Doctor,' he said. 'Don't call me, I'll call you.' Then he shrugged, 'Of course, if you'd care to enliven the journey with the story of the man that got away, I might reconsider...'

Enliven? For a glimpse of that rare smile I'd have promised anything, even laying my heart bare for his amusement, but there was no smile.

'There's nothing to tell. He wanted a rich wife so he married someone else. His mistake.'

I know, I know. Just minutes ago I'd all but issued him with a gold-edged invitation to get nosey. Now, when he'd accepted, I'd totally blown it.

I didn't really know what I was saying.

All I knew was that I so much didn't want to own up to being such a pathetic creature for the last seven years, that the lump in my throat was back and my eyes were stinging. Also I needed to blow my nose again.

'Are you starting a cold?' Gabriel asked.

'You're the doctor.'

'Runny nose, watery eyes. There are only two possibilities. You have a cold. Or you're crying.'

'Why would I be crying?' I snapped.

There was a momentary pause when he looked as if he might say something—well, *kind*. Offer me his broad shoulder in time-honoured fashion so that I could let myself go. Get it all off my chest. But he just did something with his eyebrows and said, 'It must be a cold, then.'

'Right. And what do you recommend—in your professional capacity—to alleviate the symptoms?'

'Plenty of fluids. Go to bed. Keep warm—'

'And would that be with a hot water bottle? Or are you offering the heat transfer method so recently pioneered by—'

Deep in his eyes heat flared in the darkness, for a moment burned so bright that it stopped my words. Stopped my breath.

Then he spoiled it all by saying, 'Professionally speaking—'

'No, Doctor, I want your personal opinion on that one.'

He took way too long to respond. If he'd known how unique such an invitation was from me, how many men had hoped and been disappointed, he might have been a little more excited. The hot flare in those eyes had given me hope, but in the meantime he was left hunting for some kind way to let me down. So that he wouldn't hurt me.

I'd been there so many times myself that I could read his mind as he struggled for the words. I could write the script for him. You said... Sorry, I like you, but I don't want to go to bed with you...

For that, only love would do.

I saved him the bother of hunting for the right

words. If the answer wasn't yes, I didn't want to hear it, and, checking my watch so that I could look away without being obvious about it, I said, 'If I'm going to make the most of the daylight I need to get on my way.'

'Sophie—'

But he'd waited too long, and when, finally, he managed my name it was with that apologetic hesitation that boded absolutely nothing but embarrassment for both of us. I didn't want that, so I stood up. When, like the gentleman he was, he automatically made to do the same, I shook my head, waved him back to his seat.

'No. Stay and finish your breakfast. I know where the car keys are kept.'

I didn't wait for him to offer an argument but fled the heat of the coffee bar, grateful for the frosty cold to clear my head, even if it did make my eyes sting.

I quickly loaded the dogs into the caged area at the back of the Range Rover, not wanting to be there when he returned, taking only a moment to familiarise myself with the vehicle before starting it up and backing slowly out of the garage. But my 'cold' seemed to be getting worse. The lump in my throat had grown so big that I could scarcely swallow and my eyes were swimmy. Perhaps that was why I misjudged the distance and clipped the garage door as I reversed out into the mews.

Or maybe it was because, as I checked the rearview mirror, I saw the tall, dark figure of Gabriel York, backlit by the fragile winter sunlight as he walked towards me. Or a combination of both. Whatever. My foot wobbled on the clutch, there was a loud rending of metal against wood, and for a moment I completely lost control.

Which explained why I reversed into the stone urn with the dead foliage. It hit the cobbles with a crash. The dogs yelped in fright. Then the car stalled.

The door beside me opened and Gabriel said, 'I should have guessed that your driving would be on a par with your computer skills.'

'N-no!' I protested. 'I'm a perfectly c-competent driver.' It wasn't just my foot that was shaking. My hands, hanging onto the wheel in a vice-like grip, were perfectly still but the rest of me was shivering uncontrollably. 'I've been driving since my feet c-could reach the pedals,' I said, in an attempt to convince him that, useless as I was in other directions, this incident was an aberration. 'I've n-never so much as scratched the paintwork.'

He just looked at me.

'It's true!' I yelled. And then, for absolutely no good reason, I burst into tears.

Before I could find a tissue he had his arms around me and my tears were soaking into the soft cashmere of his coat.

'No…no…' I fought the yearning to cling to him. I didn't cry. I didn't cling. Not even when Perry had explained the situation to me in words of one syllable so that even a stupid girl could understand that what I'd thought was undying love was no more than a bit of fun. The pride that had kept me dry-eyed through that nightmare had stood me in good stead ever since… 'I should make sure the dogs are okay,' I mumbled into his solid chest.

'They're fine,' he said, holding me close, not letting me go, and I gave up to the need to be held, reassured, loved…

'I'm so s-sorry, Gabriel. I don't do this…'

The words were muffled, but the sentiment must have been clear because he stroked my head. 'I know. It's just shock…'

Shock. Of course. That was all right, then.

My cheek was nestled into the hollow of his shoulder; his fingers were threaded through my hair, holding me there. Close against his heart. And then his lips brushed my forehead. It felt perfect. I'd never felt so safe and I didn't want to move. Ever. Which made it absolutely vital that I did so. Immediately. I pulled away and he made no attempt to stop me.

I slumped back into the seat and mopped up the tears, blew my nose. He left me to gather myself while he walked around the vehicle to check the damage.

'Is it bad?' I asked when he returned.

'Just a couple of dents in the bumpers. Nothing vital. No damage to the lights. Nothing to prevent your journey.' Then, 'Move over.'

'W-what?'

'Move over. You're in no fit state to drive.'

'I'm fine…' My voice wobbled a bit on 'fine'.

'No, you're not. You're worried to death about your parents, added to which you've been overdoing it with all these crazy jobs you've taken on and still finding time to rush back and check on me two or three times a day.'

'No…' Then, because he continued to look at me in a way that suggested I was wasting my breath, 'Why would I do that?'

'You do a very convincing scatterbrained blonde, Sophie, but even you couldn't have forgotten so many absolutely vital things in the last couple of weeks. Could you?' he insisted, when I didn't answer.

'I guess not. I didn't think you'd noticed.'

'It's malaria I've been suffering from, not myopia,' he said. 'You've been kind, Sophie, but it really does have to stop.'

Stop? I didn't want it to stop. Ever. Apparently I was on my own there. I'd been making a fool of myself and embarrassing him, which was why I said, '*Kind*? Oh, *please*. I'm sorry to disillusion you, but you're just another of my "crazy jobs". Your sister-in-law is *paying* me to keep an eye on you.' Not a total fib. She had offered. I just hadn't accepted. 'Make sure you don't have a relapse. Provide the occasional meal.' And, remembering my attack on the dresser with beeswax, I added, 'Do a little light dusting...'

I wanted to snatch the words back as, with his face expressionless, he voice offering not the slightest hint as to his reaction to this disclosure that my 'concern' was apparently being paid for by the hour, he said, 'Well, you give good value for money, Sophie. If you're as conscientious with all your employers it's scarcely any wonder you're exhausted. Now, move over.'

'You c-can't drive, Gabriel, you're not well.'

'On the contrary, I had the all-clear from the quack several days ago. I'm afraid you're going to have to find another job to fill the gaps in your day.'

'You didn't tell me.'

'No. He came at lunchtime, when I could be certain

you would be too busy serving food to the hungry hordes to dash home.'

'Oh, but…' But if he'd worked out that my dashes back to the mews were on his behalf, why hadn't he said anything?

'Not that it makes any difference whether I have a clean bill of health…'

Of course not. He might have recovered from the fever, but there was no way he could return to work. He couldn't do anything. No wonder he was so angry…

'…I could drive better than you when I was unconscious.'

This was clearly rubbish, but presumably meant to deal with any sympathetic feelings. He didn't want my sympathy. After that stupid outburst he wouldn't want anything from me.

But, on the point of protesting this calumny, it occurred to me that I'd got exactly what I'd been angling for back in the coffee bar. His company. So that the yawning gaps at home wouldn't seem so noticeable.

His company.

And at least he'd be getting some exercise, doing something to take his mind off his own problems instead of staring at the four walls of his kitchen and wondering if his career was over.

He climbed up beside me, handed me a pack of tissues from the door ledge and said, 'Fasten your seat belt.'

In view of the way I'd felt as he held me and comforted me, it was way too late for that, but there are times when it's wise to keep quiet and just do as you're told.

He bunched and stretched his hands a couple of times, then reached for the key and restarted the engine. With it ticking over he laid his hands lightly on the wheel. There was just the faintest tremor before he gripped it hard and hung on for a moment. Then he engaged gear and moved off. 'I take it we're heading for the M4?' he said abruptly, as he took the road west out of London.

I hadn't realised I'd been holding my breath until I tried to speak. He glanced at me.

'Yes,' I said quickly. 'The Windsor junction.'

Knightsbridge was ablaze with Christmas decorations sparkling against the pale blue sky and the thin winter sunlight. The tinsel looked out of place, wrong, somehow, needing winter darkness and snow to provide a proper seasonal setting.

'What will you do?' Gabriel's voice recalled me from an inner emptiness and I glanced at him. 'What will you do this Christmas?'

I shook my head. 'I don't want to think about it.'

'You're running out of time. You don't have friends you can go to? What about your sister?'

'Kate and Simon want to be on their own. It's their first Christmas together. And Tony, who I've always been able to rely on, has finally met the girl of his dreams and they're going to spend the holiday in the Maldives...' He'd phoned me and told me about her. He'd sounded—well, as if he didn't know what had hit him, to be honest.

'Is he the rich guy that got away?'

'Tony?' That, at least, made me smile. 'No, bless

him. Well, he's not poor, but to tell you the truth it was a bit like Buttons telling Cinderella he's fallen in love with someone else. Unexpected, but something of a relief that I don't have to feel responsible for him any more.' Then, 'But it's a good job I got a better offer and wasn't forced to camp out on his sofa. Dream girls tend to take a dim view of that.'

'You should know.'

'Me? Hell, no, I've never been anyone's dream girl, Gabriel.'

That earned me another glance—a frankly disbelieving one, which I suppose should have been flattering. Except it was the truth. 'I may have been an object of desire, or more probably lust, but I've never been the girl of any man's dreams. The one person who could put the world right with just a touch of her hand…'

My mother had done that for Dad. Just reached out, touched his arm or his cheek, and suddenly the storm clouds would lift and he'd be smiling. How could he have been so careless with such treasure? How could she have walked out on her life for a man with easy charm and a trim waist?

Maybe it wasn't just Dad. Maybe we'd all taken her for granted for too long.

'What will you do this Christmas, Gabriel? I don't suppose you'll be working?'

'No, I won't be working,' he said. 'I'll just take the dogs for a walk, defrost a ready-meal…'

'Not exactly festive.'

'I've never had a traditional family Christmas, and what you've never had you don't miss.'

'Life-saving surgery, rights for women and world peace took priority in the York household, huh?'

'It has a seasonal theme, wouldn't you say?'

'But you do that all the year. It's definitely time to give yourself a treat and indulge in some serious celebrations.'

'I wouldn't know where to start.'

'With lists. At the beginning of September,' I replied. 'Then you make the puddings and the cake. You order the free-range organic turkey and the ham. You choose the Christmas cards...'

I stopped. It was way too late to worry about any of that.

'What then?'

'After you've hit the shops and burned up your credit card buying presents for absolutely everyone you know? You have to go and find the biggest, bushiest tree that will fit in your living room and abandon all sense of taste as you load it with anything that sparkles.'

He laughed. 'Is the lack of taste essential?'

'Totally,' I began. 'No colour co-ordination allowed...'

He *laughed*! I turned to stare at him, completely knocked out by the unexpectedness of the sound. Stared at him, knocked out at the difference a few creases in a man's cheeks can make.

My silence must have warned him he'd done something odd. He glanced at me and the laughter died.

'Okay,' he said. 'Well, nothing too painful so far.'

'Don't get complacent. That's just the beginning...'

As the big four-wheel drive ate up the miles I set about entertaining Gabriel with all the hair-curling

stories—long embroidered in the years of retelling—
that made the season so memorable. I'd made him
laugh once and I'd do it again.

I gave him the one when we'd had a power cut and
had to cook, and eat, by candlelight. Very Dickensian.
Very picturesque. Very hard work.

The one where my perfect sister had over-indulged
in the pre-lunch drinks and fallen asleep with her face
in the pudding: my particular favourite.

The one when Aunt Cora had caught husband number two *in flagrante* with her best friend during a
game of Sardines on Boxing Day.

And last year, when Kate and Simon had announced they were getting married and everything
had seemed so absolutely perfect that nothing could
ever top it…

'Is this is our junction coming up?' I asked. It
wasn't, but quite suddenly I didn't feel like laughing.
And I didn't want to talk about Christmas any more.

CHAPTER NINE

GABRIEL, perhaps sensing my change of mood, put some music on the sound system and didn't speak again, except to ask for directions, until we approached the village and he was forced to stop as the congregation from the late-morning family service spilled into the street.

I was instantly spotted by the village postmistress. The last person, in fact, in the entire that world I wanted to talk to. But before I could say, Let's get out of here, and just wave back as we passed, Gabriel lowered the window.

'Sophie, dear. You're quite a stranger.' She glanced curiously at Gabriel. 'Home for Sunday lunch with your father? He's quite a stranger, too, these days.'

'Not lunch. I've just taken pity on a couple of London dogs and brought them home for a run in the country. This is their owner, Gabriel York. Gabriel, Vera runs the post office and general store. She keeps us all up to date with the news.' I hoped he'd get this code for 'village gossip'.

'Charmed,' Vera said, then, 'Have you heard from your dear mother? Is she feeling any better? Getting plenty of rest in the sun, I hope.'

Better? My father was telling people she'd gone away for her health? That wouldn't fool anyone...

'It must be so hard for your poor father, not able

to get away from the estate to be with her. Such a busy time of year.'

Or maybe all those years of good works had ring-fenced her reputation. 'Yes,' I said. 'It is.'

'We've all missed her so much. She'll be home for Christmas, I hope. She so embodies the spirit of the season, with her kindness, the way she includes everyone in her family celebrations.' She offered a hopeful smile. 'We all quite understand that she won't be able to cope this year, of course…'

Gabriel, as if he could feel me floundering, lost for words, reached across and took my hand, and, as I felt his strength pouring into me, I found myself saying, 'Of course this year it's more important than ever to make the effort. Tell everyone that we're expecting them. That they're all to join us, just as usual, won't you?'

'Really?' Her face lit up and I realised just how much they did all rely on my mother to cover the yawning emotional gaps that appeared in everyone's lives at this time of year. 'But how—?'

'I'll take care of everything.' Then self-preservation made me add, 'Actually, I could do with a little help. I'm working right through until Christmas Eve.'

'Anything, dear. We'll all be more than happy to pitch in. We never liked to offer before…' Behind us someone hooted impatiently, anxious to get home to Sunday lunch, and Vera reached out, touched my arm. 'Ring me in the week. Just tell me what you want and I'll organise everyone. Good to meet you, Gabriel.'

As we moved on I said, 'What have I done? I can't cook a turkey...'

'You can read. There are cookery books.'

'You think that's all I need do? Read a cookery book? If that's all it took we'd all be cordon bleu cooks.'

'Every journey starts with a single step.'

'Not Christmas. It starts in September and it's a route march. There are no puddings made. Or cake...'

'You can leave those to me.'

My heart leapt, but I didn't dare look at him. 'You're going to come for Christmas?'

'You looked after me. Now it's my turn.' He paused at a junction. 'We'll negotiate my hourly rate later.' Then, 'Which way?'

'Right...' I'd hoped he might have forgotten my bruising remark about taking care of him at my usual hourly rate, but clearly he hadn't. Lies, even the well-intentioned ones, came back to haunt you, and the ones that were meant to hurt deservedly came back tenfold. I vowed at that moment that I would never tell another, no matter how well intentioned, how severely provoked, and then, forcing a grin to my lips, a lightness to my voice that I was far from feeling, I said, 'Okay, but I'm not paying you as much as I earn. You can't cook.'

'Neither can you,' he reminded me. 'But I know a woman who can.' He glanced across at me. 'Of course, you'll have to find another place at your table for her.'

Forget tenfold. This was beyond numbers. 'The more the merrier,' I said, the grin—if possible—even broader, and my voice filled with all the lightness and substance of a meringue. Then, 'Turn in here.'

Dad wasn't at home, nor were the dogs.

'I expect he's taken them out,' Gabriel said, presumably putting my sudden disinclination for conversation down to unease.

'Maybe. Maybe we'll meet him out in the woods. It'll be muddy,' I said, looking doubtfully at Gabriel's town shoes. 'You'd better find a pair of boots that fit. I waved at the row of Wellingtons that lived in the mud room and, without waiting to see if he was taking my advice, kicked off my shoes and pulled on a pair that looked about my size. 'And you might want to take a waxed jacket. Brambles are hell on cashmere.'

I picked up a thumb stick and let the dogs out of the Range Rover as Gabriel joined me, looking about as far from the saturnine surgeon as it was possible to imagine in his hard-worn country clothes. He looked exactly like the man I'd always expected to spend my life with. Too bad I'd left it so long to work out that it wasn't the trappings that made the man, but the man himself.

'Let's go,' I said, and headed towards the woods, throwing sticks to distract the dogs from the pheasants which flew up in a panic at their approach.

'Tell me about the estate,' Gabriel said. 'What does your father do here?'

'Arable farming, deer, some rough shooting…' This was easier. 'He's been growing willow as a renewable energy source.' I found myself telling him about the complex issue of balancing the needs of the environment with modern farming methods—I'd been listening to my father for years, and knew a heck of a lot more than I'd thought I did—the decline of the songbird population—anything, in fact, but what I wanted to say.

That my heart was breaking.

I knew it was because it had happened to me before. But why on earth would he be interested?

And it was all right. I'd survived then and I'd survive now. But it was going to be tougher this time. Apparently it hurt more when you were older...

I slashed at a bramble blocking the path and it rebounded and caught my hand, bringing my endless chatter to an abrupt halt. Gabriel carefully disentangled me, blotted the scratch with a clean handkerchief and then looked up. 'How does that feel?'

'It stings a bit, but—'

He leaned forward and kissed me, soft and tender, on the mouth.

His lips were cold against mine, but like ice they burned, and the heat rippled through me like a volcano in the long seconds before he pulled back.

A million words flooded into my brain. Not a million different words. The same one. Again. A million times.

'How does it feel now?' he asked.

'What?' Then, 'Oh, my hand.' I'd forgotten all about my hand. 'Better...'

'Wrong answer,' he said.

'Sorry?'

'Think about it.' He took my good hand and headed back to the house. The wrong answer? Then it hit me. If I'd been on my toes, kissing it better could have been a slow, delicious, drawn-out affair. But he'd taken me by surprise…

Maybe I could have a relapse…

No. No pretence. No games. He clearly had someone else who fulfilled all his needs. Dog-carer, cook, buyer of fancy baskets of fruit. I needed to know it all. Now.

I could always have a relapse later…

'That's a very effective anaesthetic, Gabriel. Maybe you should patent it.'

'Kissing it better is as old as time.'

Not like that, it wasn't…

'Let's get back and get that cleaned up properly. If your hand gets infected you won't be much use on the twenty-fifth.'

Okay, we were back to Christmas. Exactly the opening I'd been looking for. 'Tell me about this cook of yours,' I demanded.

He glanced at me. Well, maybe I had been a bit fierce. 'June?'

'Yes,' I said, before I could lose my nerve. 'Tell me about June.'

'She was a theatre nurse.'

Of course. All that eye contact over the operating table…

'More than that—' *No!* 'A great theatre nurse. Unfortunately she was hurt in a car accident and had to give up work.'

Oh, great. I couldn't even hate her…

'That's tough,' I said.

'Yes, but she's a fighter, and she's always loved to cook. She doesn't need the money—she received substantial compensation—but she likes to keep busy, so she set up a small catering business.'

'And she takes care of your dogs when you go away as a little sideline?'

He stopped, blocking the path. 'Jealous?'

About to do the whole 'Excuse me and why on earth would I be jealous of her taking care of your dogs?' bit, I remembered my vow. No more pretence. No more lies.

'Jealous as hell,' I said.

'Good.' And then he kissed me again, taking his time about it. He tilted my chin up with the edge of his thumb, his cold fingers stroking against my neck as he looked at me with those bottomless eyes for what seemed like a century. 'I'm really glad about that,' he said, his voice low and husky and thick with need as he slowly lowered his mouth to mine.

He'd kissed me before. Hot and hard. Cold and sweet.

This was different. I'd never been kissed like this before. It was as if he was giving me a part of him that he hadn't even known existed, and something so deep inside me that I'd forgotten it was there responded and answered him with everything I had to offer.

It was as if I'd been living in glass box for years. I could see everything that was happening around me but I was detached, apart. Nothing had been able to touch me until now, without warning, the glass had been shattered and noise and colour and life were rushing in, bludgeoning my heightened senses.

The touch of Gabriel's hands as they held my face, his thumbs brushing my cheeks, cold-on-cold. Leaves rustled around our feet as the wind stirred them. The scent of his skin, touched by the clean wind.

This went way beyond kissing me better.

He had told me he'd show me how to give the kiss of life. And this was it.

It left me clinging to him. Weak, trembling from head to toe, but undoubtedly alive.

And then there was a clatter of pheasants' wings and the dogs, stupid things, came careering out of the woods, expecting to be told how brilliant they were.

Gabriel held me for a moment, face as grave as it had ever been. Then he smiled and said, 'You'll like June.'

I thought he was being overly optimistic, frankly, but I loved him, so I left him with his illusions and said, 'Of course I will.' Then, because I didn't want to tempt fate, I added, 'I'll do my best, anyway. But right now I think we'd better leave these birds in peace.'

I set off briskly for the house as Gabriel whistled the dogs to heel, but he caught me, took my arm, tucked it beneath his. Then, as we passed the tree nursery, he stopped. 'What's this?'

'The Christmas tree farm.'

'This is where you pick the biggest, bushiest tree you can find?'

'The very place.'

'Well, hadn't we'd better go pick out a Christmas tree?'

'I think we need to get back. I'm worried about Dad.' Then, because even from the road I could see the one I'd pick, I said, 'Okay. That one.'

*   *   *

Dad still wasn't there when we got back, and I went upstairs and stuck a dressing on my hand while Gabriel gave the dogs some water. It wasn't that I didn't want a repeat of the kissing it better thing. I just needed to concentrate on one problem at a time.

Returning to the kitchen, I opened the fridge, checking to see what was there, making sure that he was eating. It was worse than I'd thought. There was nothing, not even milk.

'I was going to ask if you're hungry,' I said to Gabriel as he joined me, putting his hand on my shoulder as he looked over my head.

'Actually, I'm famished, but it looks as if I'm going to have to buy you lunch as well as breakfast.'

'It's too late. The pub stops serving lunch at two.'

'The motorway services never close,' he pointed out.

In reply, I opened a cupboard and found a couple of cans of soup. He took them from me and opened them while I dug around in the freezer for some of my mother's home-made bread rolls. I stuck some in the Aga and within minutes the kitchen smelled enough like home to make me wish I'd taken the motorway services option.

'How many people are we going to be catering for?'

'What?' I dragged myself back to the present. To reality. Trying not to let my heart get in a giddy state about that 'we'. This was a man who'd spent his life avoiding hurting other people by refusing to get involved. Mr No Commitment. He'd never lied. Never pretended. He was straight down the line. Absolutely serious. And I was going to have to let him go without a backward glance. But I would have Christmas. I would be his gift from me. He would be my gift to myself.

'Guests? For Christmas Day?' he prompted, while my mind was freewheeling.

'Oh, right. Well, usually about twenty. But Mum won't be here, and I don't suppose Aunt Cora will come unless she wants to take the opportunity to glare at Dad. Kate and Simon won't be here, nor will Tony, but you and your lady cook will fill a couple of gaps.'

'Sophie—'

'What?'

'I heard a car.'

It was Dad. He had his Labradors at his heels and he was carrying Flossie, my mother's old spaniel, in his arms. Percy and Joe sat respectfully, keeping their distance. He didn't evoke any surprise at seeing me. Just said, 'I took her to the vet. There's nothing he can do. She's pining for your mother.'

All the anger, all the rage I'd been feeling for weeks, just washed away from me and I went and put my arms around him. 'Go and find her, Dad. Tell her how much you need her.'

'But I can't leave. The farm...'

'You've got a manager to take care of the day-to-day running of the place.'

'The dogs...'

He was afraid, I realised. Scared she wouldn't come.

'We'll take care of them,' Gabriel said without hesitation.

It said much for Dad's state of mind that he didn't

even query this offer from a total stranger. He just looked at me and said, 'Do you think she'll listen?'

'You'll never know unless you try.'

I packed him a bag while Gabriel booked him a flight. He came upstairs to find me and give me the details.

'I've booked him on a flight leaving this evening,' he began.

'Gabriel, it's impossible. We can't take all these dogs back to London. I'll have to stay here,' I said, desperate because I couldn't let all those other people down, either. Desperate because I didn't want to leave him.

'No, Sophie. Take your father to the airport. I'll stay here. Keep an eye on things. I'll take good care of Flossie, I promise.'

'Well, that deals with one of the desperates,' I said, under my breath. 'There's plenty of transport—you'll find all the keys in the office. And you'll be looked after. I'll phone Mrs Marsh, the daily, to warn her you'll be here. She'll cook for you.' Then, 'Unless, of course, you'd rather have…' I found I couldn't bring myself to say June '…someone else.'

'I'll be fine,' he said, and held me briefly. Which didn't exactly answer the unasked question. 'Now, you'd better go or your father will miss his flight. Call me when you get home.'

The thing about Christmas is that once you open up and decide to enjoy it, it seems to take on a life of its own. I asked Mrs Andrews, of course, and since it was obvious that Alan from the toy store was going to be on his own I asked him to join us, too. There was plenty of room in the Range Rover.

And when I found Greta breaking her heart because she didn't have the money to give her girls everything she wanted, I thought, What the heck? The more the merrier. We could all squeeze in somehow, and what was Christmas without children?

Then, when I called in at the agency to sort out a few things, and asked Miss Frosty—Lucy—what she was doing for the holiday, instead of snapping at me she burst into tears and told me all about how she'd split up with the man she'd been living with for years. Fortunately she had her own car, because the Range Rover was getting to be a bit of a squeeze.

Gabriel drove up for the Nativity play. As we sat together in church and watched the story unfold, heard the children sing the carols, my eyes filled with tears.

I hoped he hadn't seen, but he took my hand and held it. He didn't need to say anything. Afterwards we had supper with Lucia and her family, and then walked back to the mews cottage.

With his fingers laced through mine, I felt emboldened enough to turn and say to him, 'Please don't drive back tonight.' He couldn't possibly have mistaken my meaning.

'I have to. I left Vera babysitting Flossie.' He kissed my cheek. 'I'll be back on Christmas Eve, to help transport your waifs and strays.'

'Drive carefully,' I said, letting him go. Please drive carefully...

* * *

On Christmas Eve, after I'd served my last portion of turkey at the pub, I made a detour to see Paul, the homeless guy with the little dog, who sold the *Big Issue* near the underground station. I hadn't seen him for a couple of weeks, and I wanted to deliver a couple of tins of food for the pup's Christmas dinner.

'Have you heard anything about a flat,' I asked, as I made a fuss of the little mongrel.

'New job, new flat,' he said, pleased as punch. 'Right after Christmas.'

After Christmas.

Well, I knew what my mother would do. Not that it mattered. I invited him to spend Christmas with us because it was what *I* would do, and took him back to the mews and introduced him to Gabriel, who'd already arrived and, having got Tigger crated up, was busy packing the stuff I'd left out to take home with me into the rear of the Rover.

'I've missed you,' he said quietly, after I'd introduced him to Paul. And he briefly took my hand. His eyes said how much. Or maybe it was just a reflection of my own need.

'You look a lot better,' I said.

'I feel better. Walking the dogs has helped. And I've made some decisions about my future.' He had that ready-for-action look of a man with his sights set on a distance horizon and I was seized with fear. 'I'll tell you later,' he said.

'Any news from Dad?' I asked, hoping to disguise the fact that 'later' seemed like for ever.

'There's still time.'

'How's Flossie?'

'Holding on.'

*   *   *

Mrs Marsh and Vera had done us proud. The house was gleaming, the fridge and freezer were loaded, and there was a note on the kitchen table to tell me that they'd be arriving early to start vegetable duty the following morning.

Only the decorations were missing. And my parents.

'Where are they, Gabriel? I phoned; I sent a text…' No one was answering.

He opened his arms and I went into them. Just for a moment. Then I took a deep breath, found a smile, and said, 'Okay. I can do this.'

'Of course you can.'

He left me organising supper for everyone while he lit the fire in the drawing room and then organised for the other men to bring in the luggage and boxes from the cars, sorted out the bedrooms. By the time everyone had finished, and Gabriel had opened a bottle of something old, warming and festive from a hamper he'd brought with him, the kitchen was filled with the scent of potatoes baking to go with the ham.

'Relax, your dad won't let you down,' he said, as he handed me a glass.

'No.' I sounded more convinced than I was, but the festive cheer was trickling down to warm all the chilly corners of my heart and it was beginning to feel a little bit more like Christmas. Then another car arrived. Lucy or June?

Gabriel went out to help with the bags while I went back to rolling pastry for little fruit tarts. And when I looked again it was to see Gabriel with his arms enfolding a small woman who was completely hidden.

Was I jealous?

Too right.

It stabbed through me, sharp and poisonous, and then Gabriel straightened, turned, and said, 'Sophie, I'd like you to meet June.'

June was a slight, elegant woman in tight jeans and a floppy sweatshirt, with short, spiky silver hair. And she was sixty if she was a day. Gabriel caught my jaw-drop moment as introduced her, smiling at me over her head.

Bastard! He knew exactly what I'd been thinking and he'd let me go on thinking it…

It was perhaps as well for him that, having welcomed my guest with an enthusiasm that she might have found a little bit over the top, I was distracted by the arrival of Lucy. And then Greta's little girls, apprehensive and shy in a strange house full of people they didn't know, came downstairs from their bedroom, clinging to their mother's skirt. I loaded them up with the box of decorations I'd asked Gabriel to bring down from attic and despatched them with their mother and Alan to blitz the house with tinsel, then, while Gabriel showed June to her room, Lucy and I laid out supper in the kitchen.

'You were right,' she said, as I checked the potatoes and hoped I'd done enough. 'You do have domestic skills.'

I was saved from having to respond to this unlikely compliment by a rush of cold air as the back door was flung open, and I turned to see Gabriel with the thickest, bushiest bunch of mistletoe I'd ever seen.

'I thought you were taking it easy with June,' I said meaningfully. Then, 'Where did you get that?'

'I saw it when we were in the woods last week. I meant to get it earlier, but Vera arrived...'

For a moment I was speechless. 'You went out there in the dark?' I was furious. 'You could have fallen. Been hurt. No one would have known where you were—'

'I eat plenty of carrots,' he said, grinning as he cut me off in full vent, and I realised that I'd totally betrayed myself. That I was emotionally naked... 'Where do you want it?' he asked.

'Just hold it right there for the moment.'

'Here?' He looked up, as if expecting to see a beam above him.

'That's it. Maybe a little higher...higher... Perfect.' And then I kissed him. Once you were emotionally naked there was no point in playing it cool. Actually, I'd meant just to touch his lips with mine, but the mistletoe magic must have been particularly strong because the kiss seemed to go on and on, an unbreakable enchantment that enfolded us, isolated us—

'Hey, don't keep that gorgeous stuff to yourselves, you two!'

I pulled away to the laughter of a kitchen full of the people I'd gathered together. 'I've missed you,' I said, so that only he could hear. Then, louder, '*Excellent* mistletoe...'

And into those two words I put everything else I wanted to say to him but couldn't right there in the kitchen, with everyone looking on, which was probably a good thing. It would be absolutely fatal to risk letting slip those three little words 'I love you' to a man who'd apparently erased 'commitment' from his dictionary. He'd probably run a mile.

As it was, he simply put out a cold hand, touched my cheek. 'Ten out of ten,' he agreed.

It was all it took to make the world seem like a magic place as the air filled with the warm scent of spiced wine, baking potatoes and warm bread.

'All we need now,' I said, 'is snow.'

We got the next best thing. Aunt Cora.

Supper was a riot. Too much food, too much everything. And, at the far end of the table, Gabriel. A man with his future all decided. Was there going to be any part in it for me?

'What are you doing?'

It was late. I'd had to wait for everyone to settle down before I could hang up the stockings along the mantel. One for everyone, each with an orange, some nuts, chocolate money, a sherbet dab, a pocket diary and a bath fizzer, plus all the other silly little gifts that had been a part of our family Christmas for as long as I could remember. It was the first time I'd done them and I discovered it was as much fun as— no, more fun than getting one.

'Playing Santa Claus. You are supposed to be in bed,' I said.

'And this?' He picked up the gift I'd wrapped for him. I'd stuck on a big label that said *'Not to be opened until Christmas'*.

He ignored it, pulling at the ribbon.

'Hey! You can't do that!' I said, pointing at the label.

'I've got news for you, my love,' he said, as the clock on the mantel began to chime, and, grinning like a big kid, he tore the paper. 'It is Christmas...' The words faltered as a silk négligée slipped from the paper. Palest oyster silk. Size eight. 'I think there's been some mistake, here,' he said.

'No. No mistake.' I took it from him. I'd meant this for tomorrow night, but all evening I'd been melting with desire, wishing we were on our own... 'Come on, I'll show you how it works.'

I took his hand and led him up the stairs to my bedroom, and, leaving him standing in the middle of the room, said, 'Wait there. I'll be right back.'

It was entirely possible that by now he'd got the idea. But when I opened the bathroom door, wearing nothing but the négligée and Chanel No 5, I realised with delight that for once he was the one rendered speechless. So I put my arms around his neck and said, 'Happy Christmas, Gabriel.'

'I don't know what to say.'

'You don't have to say anything. All you have to do is open your present.' And then I kissed him and he pulled me into his arms. I could tell he wasn't going to need any further encouragement.

I was woken by a shattering noise, but as I disentangled myself from Gabriel's arms and grabbed for the alarm clock I realised that the sound was coming from downstairs.

I flung back the covers, grabbed a wrap, and with Gabriel hard on my heels rushed into the drawing room. The girls were there. One of them was screaming. The other was motionless, not breathing, her face swollen.

'Peanuts,' he said, spotting an open packet raided from the cupboard as he scooped her up and carried her through to the kitchen. 'She's gone into anaphylactic shock. I need a sharp knife and a ballpoint pen or a straw.'

'What's happening? What's wrong?' Greta shrieked as she came flying down the stairs to join us.

'Go and start the car, please, Greta,' Gabriel said, ice-cool, and when she would have ignored him, to rush to her little girl, I grabbed the Range Rover keys from the dresser and thrust them into her hand.

'He's a doctor. Go and get the car started. Use the phone to call the local hospital and tell them we're coming in with her.' And, when she still hesitated, 'Now!'

She fled. And I turned in time to see Gabriel plunge a small sharp knife into the child's windpipe. 'Take the refill out of that pen,' he said, without looking up. My hands were shaking so much that the simple task seemed beyond me, but it came free and he used the plastic tube to keep the incision open so that he could blow air into the child's lungs...

There was a nightmare drive to the cottage hospital, and a nightmare wait for the swelling to reduce in response to the antihistamine. Then she was cleaned up, stitched and put to bed.

And I was *still* shaking.

Gabriel was like a rock.

'You said you'd show me how to give the kiss of life. That was a bit closer than I ever want to come

again,' I said, trying to hold onto the cup of tea someone had given me without spilling it.

'You don't need lessons, Sophie. Just being in your
company is enough to breathe life into the most mor-
ibund of hearts.' He reached out, took the cup from
me and held my face between his hands. 'Tell Lucy
to take you off her books,' he said. 'I'm employing
you for the rest of your life. I may not need a wife,
but I sure as hell need you.'

What? *No-o-o.* It took me a moment to reply—
employing me! 'You've already had me. Unlike a
puppy, I'm just for Christmas.' What else could I say
to a man of no commitment?

But then, with perfect timing, Greta walked in. 'Gabriel, Sophie... How can I ever thank you both?' She
looked flattened, shell-shocked. 'I had no idea...'

Gabriel, who, I'm happy to say, looked a touch
shell-shocked himself, tore his gaze from my face and
said, 'These things sometimes flare up without any
warning. The hospital will give her a special device
to keep with her at all times. Show her how to use it.
Explain how to live with the allergy. They'll probably
let her out in an hour or two. Just as soon as they're
sure she's stable.'

'We'll get someone to come over with some
clothes for you and bring you back,' I said through a
sort of creeping numbness. My mind wasn't really on
the conversation at hand, but on one a lot more personal to me—and Gabriel. *How could he say that?*
How was I going to get through the rest of the day?
Somehow... 'But I have to get back. If I don't get
the turkey on soon no one is going eat before night-
fall...'

Gabriel butted in. 'Stuff the turkey! I've got something to say to you and it's more important than any turkey—'

He grabbed my hand and, ignoring Greta, a couple of nurses who'd gathered by the drinks machine and a number of sorry-looking patients waiting to be seen by the doctor, dragged me into the nearest cubicle. 'What the hell do you mean "just for Christmas"?'

There was no way on earth this conversation wasn't being shared with everyone on the other side of the curtain.

'Gabriel,' I said, as quietly as I could. 'You don't do commitment. You just said it. You don't need a wife—'

'I was wrong. I didn't mean… Sophie, I'm going back to Africa—'

Wrong?

'Oh, I see,' I said, cutting him off. 'You need me to sort out the details, is that it? Find you a compatible anti-malaria drug? Make sure you take it—'

Okay, I was beginning to get the picture. He *needed* me. Well, he'd got me—even if it was going to be in Africa—but first he was going to have to pay for that 'employing you for the rest of your life'. That had *not* been romantic…

'No!' He ran his fingers through his uncombed hair and said, 'No, damn it. I need you. Just to be there to come home to. Just to be there to reach out and touch when the world seems a dark place. Just to hold…'

He stopped, struggling to put exactly what he was feeling into words.

'Gabriel, it's okay…'

That was romantic enough. I wanted to get to the rest of our lives now…

'No, it's not okay. I have to tell you this. You thought you'd given me the kiss of life, Sophie? Well, I'm telling you that you've turned my heart from an efficient pump into something that beats faster whenever I think of you. And I think of you constantly. You've warmed my heart and my spirit and the simple truth is that I cannot imagine living without you,' he said.

'What are you saying, Gabriel?'

He reached out then, cradled my cheek in the palm of his hand. 'I'm saying that I love you, Sophie.'

From beyond the curtain a cheer went up.

He glanced briefly towards the commotion, then smiled. 'I love you, and despite the fact that you've already told me that you don't need a husband I'd like you to give some serious consideration to the idea. Not because I need someone to take care of me, or even because you need someone to take care of you, but because together we will be so much greater than the sum of our two parts. Marry me, Sophie.'

Now I was the one struggling for words. 'You shouldn't say things like that on the spur of the moment,' I said. 'I might take you seriously.'

He reached into the pocket of the trousers he'd pulled on even as he'd plunged down the stairs back at the house. 'Not the spur of the moment.' And he produced a small box. 'I bought this when I came up to London last week. I know it fits because I borrowed one of your rings…' He opened the box, slid the ring onto my finger. 'A diamond is for ever, Sophie, and whatever else I do in my life I want you beside me that long. For ever.'

'This is all part of the macho York thing, isn't it? When you go for something, you don't quit.' *Please.* 'There's absolutely no point in me playing hard to get, is there?'

The smile deepened. 'Well, you can try,' he offered. 'But after last night I'd have said it was a bit late—'

'Shh! Everyone's listening.'

'Then you'd better hurry up and say yes, or I'll tell them exactly how you seduced me...'

I'd already had a master class in how to shut someone up. I put it to good use and kissed him, long and hard.

After what seemed like an age, I pulled away. 'I have a confession to make,' I said, fighting to get my breath back. 'But I'll tell you in the car.' I'd eventually remembered the turkey and had to get back to the house. Pronto.

'Confess away,' he said, once we'd settled ourselves into the car.

'Crissie did give me some money to look after you—told Lucy to pay me for the hours I worked. I wouldn't let her. I put the cash in an envelope and put it back through her letterbox.'

'Tell me something I don't know.'

'But—'

'I notice when bills don't arrive and I called the agency. Lucy told me you'd paid the dog-walking account yourself.'

'Why didn't you say?'

'I thought you'd tell me yourself, eventually. And I was right.'

'Know-it-all. I knew you wouldn't take rent from me, but I couldn't deprive the agency of their fee.'

'You are something else, Sophie.' He pulled into the drive, reached across and took my hand, spreading out my fingers beneath his. 'Something very special.'

'Of course I am. It takes a special woman to ride the slip-stream and hold on long enough to catch a York man.' I moved my hand so that the diamond flashed in the low, slanting rays of the sun. And then I realised something. 'The tremor. It's gone!'

'Days ago. The minute I realised that it wouldn't actually be the end of my life if I couldn't be a surgeon. I'm not just a surgeon, I'm a doctor, and I still have something useful to offer. That's when I asked the medical charity if they'd take me on permanently. It's time to put something back, Sophie. You do understand?' He grasped my hand, held it tight. 'It won't be easy. I know I'm being selfish, taking you with me.'

'Just try and leave without me.' I lifted his hand to my lips and kissed it. 'But right now I have a house full of guests to feed.'

Except I didn't.

At home, Vera was in charge of the vegetables, Mrs Andrews was in charge of the sherry, and my mother was in her rightful place—in charge of the turkey. It seemed so right, her being there, that I almost forgot she'd been away.

She finished basting the bird, closed the cooker door and came and gave me a hug that didn't need words. It said, Well done. And I'm proud of you. And

I'm happy to be home. No words needed. Well, maybe just a few—

'Mum, this is Gabriel York. He's been looking after Flossie for you.' Flossie looked up at the sound of her name and wagged her tail. 'We're getting married and going to work in Africa. Together.'

'That sounds exciting,' she said. And gave him a hug, too.

We went in search of Dad and found Kate and Simon in the dining room, laying the table. 'She forgot to defrost the turkey,' Simon said with a grin, and got a slap with a cracker for his cheek.

Dad was in the drawing room, looking a bit jet-lagged, but he roused himself to say, 'I got it all wrong about the golfer, you know. She just wanted to get away. Have some time to herself.'

'Take care of her, okay. And give her a hand putting the garden back together.'

'Absolutely. Anything she wants.'

'I think we're surplus to requirements here,' Gabriel murmured in my ear. 'Let's go and take a shower. I've got a little Christmas present for you…'

It was a ticket to St Lucia; he'd bought one for himself, too. 'And then I want to have another look at my Christmas present from you…'

The wedding wasn't the way I'd planned it all those years ago. We didn't have time to wait while all that stuff was organised. Besides, my mother was too busy rebuilding her garden and she was doing enough looking after Percy, Joe and Tigger while we were away.

We just had a quiet service in the village church,

with Ginny as my 'best woman' and a party at home for our friends and family.

Of course the flowers were spectacular…totally in keeping with my TFB status. But that was my only concession to fantasy. This marriage had nothing to do with fantasy. It was solid, based on truth, honour and the kind of love that isn't about staring into one another's eyes across a candlelit table but facing in the same direction, moving forward together.

Besides, I had much better things to do with the money my father had saved on a fancy marquee and a thousand guests. A new medical centre with my mother's name on it in an African village, for a start.

It was just the beginning.

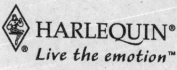

Do you like stories that get *up close* and *personal*?
Do you long to be loved *truly, madly, deeply...*?

If you're looking for emotionally intense, tantalizingly tender love stories, stop searching and start reading

Harlequin Romance®

You'll find authors who'll leave you breathless, including:

Liz Fielding
Winner of the 2001 RITA Award for
Best Traditional Romance
(The Best Man and the Bridesmaid)

Day Leclaire
USA *Today* bestselling author

Leigh Michaels
Bestselling author with 30 million
copies of her books sold worldwide

Renee Roszel
USA *Today* bestselling author

Margaret Way
Australian star with 80 novels to her credit

Sophie Weston
A fresh British voice and a hot talent!

Don't miss their latest novels, coming soon!

HARLEQUIN®
Makes any time special®

If you enjoyed what you just read,
then we've got an offer you can't resist!

Take 2 bestselling
love stories FREE!
Plus get a FREE surprise gift!

Clip this page and mail it to Harlequin Reader Service®

IN U.S.A.	IN CANADA
3010 Walden Ave.	P.O. Box 609
P.O. Box 1867	Fort Erie, Ontario
Buffalo, N.Y. 14240-1867	L2A 5X3

YES! Please send me 2 free Harlequin Romance® novels and my free surprise gift. After receiving them, if I don't wish to receive anymore, I can return the shipping statement marked cancel. If I don't cancel, I will receive 6 brand-new novels every month, before they're available in stores! In the U.S.A., bill me at the bargain price of $3.57 plus 25¢ shipping & handling per book and applicable sales tax, if any*. In Canada, bill me at the bargain price of $4.05 plus 25¢ shipping & handling per book and applicable taxes**. That's the complete price and a savings of 10% off the cover prices—what a great deal! I understand that accepting the 2 free books and gift places me under no obligation ever to buy any books. I can always return a shipment and cancel at any time. Even if I never buy another book from Harlequin, the 2 free books and gift are mine to keep forever.

186 HDN DZ72
386 HDN DZ73

Name	(PLEASE PRINT)	
Address	Apt.#	
City	State/Prov.	Zip/Postal Code

Not valid to current Harlequin Romance® subscribers.
Want to try another series? Call 1-800-873-8635
or visit www.morefreebooks.com.

* Terms and prices subject to change without notice. Sales tax applicable in N.Y.
** Canadian residents will be charged applicable provincial taxes and GST.
All orders subject to approval. Offer limited to one per household.
® are registered trademarks owned and used by the trademark owner and its licensee.

HROM04R   ©2004 Harlequin Enterprises Limited

eHARLEQUIN.com
The Ultimate Destination for Women's Fiction

Visit eHarlequin.com's Bookstore today
for today's most popular books at great prices.

- An extensive selection of romance books by top authors!

- Choose our convenient "bill me" option. No credit card required.

- New releases, Themed Collections and hard-to-find backlist.

- A sneak peek at upcoming books.

- Check out book excerpts, book summaries and Reader Recommendations from other members and post your own too.

- Find out what everybody's reading in Bestsellers.

- Save BIG with everyday discounts and exclusive online offers!

- Our Category Legend will help you select reading that's exactly right for you!

- Visit our Bargain Outlet often for huge savings and special offers!

- Sweepstakes offers. Enter for your chance to win special prizes, autographed books and more.

**Your purchases are 100%
guaranteed—so shop online
at www.eHarlequin.com today!**

Like a phantom in the night comes
a new promotion from

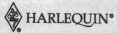
HARLEQUIN®

INTRIGUE®

GOTHIC ROMANCE

Beginning in August 2004, we offer you
a classic blend of chilling suspense and
electrifying romance, starting with....

A DANGEROUS INHERITANCE
LEONA KARR

And don't miss a spine-tingling Eclipse tale each month!